BROTHER
DUMB

BROTHER
DUMB

SKY GILBERT

MISFIT

ECW Press

Published by ECW PRESS, 2120 Queen Street East, Suite 200,
Toronto, Ontario, Canada M4E 1E2

LIBRARY AND ARCHIVES CANADA CATALOGUING IN PUBLICATION

Gilbert, Sky
Brother Dumb / Sky Gilbert.

ISBN-13: 978-1-55022-768-0
ISBN-10: 1-55022-768-8

I. Title.

PS8563.I4743B76 2007   C813'.54   C2006-906637-X

Editor for the press: Michael Holmes
Production: Mary Bowness
Author Photo: David Hawe
Printing: Friesens

The publication of *Brother Dumb* has been generously supported by the
Canada Council, the Ontario Arts Council, and the Government
of Canada through the Book Publishing Industry
Development Program.

DISTRIBUTION
CANADA: Jaguar Book Group, 100 Armstrong Ave., Georgetown, ON, L7G 5S4

PRINTED AND BOUND IN CANADA

ECW PRESS
ecwpress.com

for Ian

The unexamined life is not worth living.

— SOCRATES

If I'm going to tell you about it, I have to start back in 1951, with the black apartment and the black sheets. At the time I was being melodramatic, but for good reason. Like Masha in *The Three Sisters* I was in mourning for my life. Or perhaps I should say I was in mourning for someone else's life, for the life of the main character in my first novel.

It was strange, the way I wrote the damn thing. I started it, or at least started writing about the character, before I went off to war, and then wrote some of it while the war was on, and then some after. Around the time I got the black apartment I was coming to terms with the fact that the novel was going to be over, and there wasn't going to be anything more for me to write about the character. That is, I'd written the character out. Or perhaps that isn't an accurate thing to say. The feeling wasn't exactly that I had written the character out, because the guy had become much more real to me than that. I had the feeling he was my best friend, the best friend I'd never had, and I was having real trouble saying goodbye. I was certain that he had another life after the novel, a life that he was continuing to live — only I wasn't invited to participate. I know it's a concept that's pretty hard to get your mind around, but if you're a writer you might understand.

I don't think it's completely crazy to think that characters in novels have lives of their own. If you want some intellectual justification for the concept all you have to do is go back to old Scaligero, a medieval scholar who was a great classifier — he was even worse than Aristotle in that respect — really into naming things, into ordering the universe. Strangely enough, for such an anal-retentive guy, he was also really sensitive to great literature. At one point when talking about what reality is and is not, he suggested that the characters the poet Virgil had created were actually real, that they actually lived. He said, anyway, that they were more real than reality itself, because they were so beautiful.

Now, I'm not saying the character I created was that beautiful, but what I am saying is that he was beautiful to me. Actually, talking about it like this feels a little strange. I begin to sound like a flit. I guess the best way to describe it would be to say that the character was like the brother I never had. He thought like I did, and generally behaved like I did, liked the things I liked, hated the things I hated. Except, naturally, he wasn't me. The punishment for having created a character that is so alive for you, and such a great pal, is that when you have to say goodbye, you don't want to. Ultimately you can't believe he's gone. It's not like you can go back to your own book and read it again, like other people can, and get reacquainted. It's just not possible. The experience of creating a character is not the same as reading about him. If you read about characters in a book, when you get lonely for them you can read the book again. But no experience can ever compare to giving birth to a character. That's what it's like, giving birth. It's the closest you'll ever get to another human being, real or not.

All this was clear to me at the time, crystal clear. I was like a parent saying goodbye to a child, or a lover breaking up with a beautiful girl. Jesus, I've been in that situation too many times. The worst thing about saying goodbye to a beautiful girl is thinking about some other guy with her. No matter how much you hate her, how she drives you nuts, and even if you think she's stupid and you want to throttle her, when it's over you only remember the good times — like when she was eating some crazy food like sardines, or she made you french fries that were really tasty, or the way she said "I love you" when you asked her to, on cue, and it always came out right. And then you imagine her eating sardines in front of some creepy guy, some fat jerk — or worse, some skinny little critic with glasses, some guy who thinks your writing is fundamentally flawed or even "quixotic." Maybe you imagine him kissing her neck — assuming she had a fabulous neck — and you want to die, the feeling is so bad.

This was the state I was in. I had this feeling in the pit of my stomach like someone had punched me, all because this character wasn't going to be my friend anymore. It wasn't something I could go to a psychiatrist about. Really, what would I say? *I have to say goodbye to a character who's going to go on living his life without me?* I think they'd figure I was certifiable for sure. Guys have been put away for less. Anyway, there was no one I could go to, no one I could talk to about this because it was so wacky.

On top of it, I wasn't really trying to get rid of the hurt.

This, again, is how it was similar to ending an affair. There are times after you break up with someone — or are broken up with — when you definitely should be forgetting about the whole thing and moving on, but, on purpose, you're not. You're doing exactly what you shouldn't be doing; you're nurturing all the pain, all the hurt. Why? Because you know that when the hurt goes away, then the last connection you have with that loved person is gone too.

The whole situation was made a lot worse by jazz. I know it sounds strange, but this time in my life probably pretty well accounts for my lifelong aversion to the style. Okay, that's not really true. What irritates me is the concept of jazz. But I don't like even talking about words like "style" and "concept" when I think of jazz because they don't apply. Forgive me if you're a jazz fan, but I really do think the whole thing is bogus.

Now there are two different kinds of jazz. There's the kind of jazz that isn't jazz — which is okay, I guess — but it's not jazz. And then there's jazz itself, which is pretentious, and lousy, and generally stupid. I should explain. The jazz that is not jazz is when a guy plays some tune on the piano, a tune he didn't even write, a tune in the public domain, and then adds some little doodads and gee-jobs here and there, some trills, and scales, and whatever else tickles his goddamn fancy. In other words, it involves playing around and so-called improvising with what is already written. The only problem is that the only thing good about this type of so-called jazz is the tune itself, the tune somebody else wrote. What you are doing, listening to the so-called jazz musician, is straining to hear the tune you can barely hear because the guy is fooling around with it like crazy and ruining your experience of the tune — because all you'd like to do is just hear it for Christ's sake. So this type of so-called jazz is manipulative. It fools you into thinking you like it when all you like is something that the musician *isn't* doing.

Then there's the second type of jazz. It's much worse, and has pretty much taken over these days, because the first type of jazz is now considered old-fashioned. This second kind is epitomized by Miles Davis. And yeah, I guess they can call it jazz if they want to, because it is, essentially, unlistenable. You can go on all you want to about Miles Davis — what a genius he is, how nobody can match him — but wake up and smell the coffee. It just sounds like noise. There is no tune, no music, nothing. It's as bad as modern, avant-garde classical music — which is why the eggheads like it. God help you if you try to hum it — hummable would be too commercial. Anyway, this Miles Davis type of jazz is unbelievably pretentious, and people like to sit around for hours with their eyes closed snapping their fingers saying, "Oh yeah, this part, you've got to listen to this part, it's so fabulous, so perfect, so beautiful." And you listen to it and it's just noise. It makes perfect sense that this kind of jazz came along. It's perfect for all the pseudo artists. They can become experts at it. It doesn't require taste or discernment — all you have to do is memorize the names of all the gods of jazz and then go on about the recordings, like the one by Miles Davis called *Awake in Spain* or something. Anyway, it's about Spain — except it isn't. All you have to do is go on and on about these records and you become an instant expert. Pretentious people love it.

And these jazz clubs, they are the worst. Just a bunch of people sitting around congratulating themselves on how musically savvy they are, and adoring their icons, the jazz musicians, who are usually stoned out of their minds and not very talented. I know you might think it's petty or ungenerous of me to hate jazz so much but it's the way I feel. And remember, I'm not talking about any of the real so-called jazz greats like Ella Fitzgerald or Dinah Washington. These gals knew how to sing tunes; they were not singing jazz really. Ella had to do that scat stuff to please the aficionados — the doo-wat doo-wat stuff — so they could imagine they were listening to the real ponderous thing.

To get back to my story, jazz was just beginning to get big in Greenwich Village at the time, and they had all these little clubs where people like Charlie Parker would play, and I couldn't have been more turned off by the whole production. This was a problem because the one thing that would have gotten me out of my funk would have been to go out at night and, you know, have a cigarette and a drink in one of these clubs and meet some beautiful jazz gal, but I couldn't stand it. I'm sure they would have been cute in their little turtlenecks — turtlenecks were in vogue. But I knew I would have gotten all excited about one of these cute things only to find out she was really into Miles Davis, and it would have made me want to vomit.

So what did I do? Perversely, I turned my apartment into kind of a jazz club. That is, it was all black anyway, like the clubs, and you got to it by going down a basement stairway at the front of the house. There were just two rooms: one big one at the front and then a smaller room at the back that was my study, where I finished working on my book. I liked that little study because there were no windows at all. There was a tiny grate, but it was all boarded up. I could work in there in complete silence and solitude. There was nothing in there but a desk and a typewriter. The front room was different; it had the bed with the black sheets.

Now I knew the black sheets were intimidating. Women probably thought I was some sort of sex sorcerer or something, and nothing could be further from the truth. I'm an ordinary guy in that department, too ordinary probably. Maybe it's why so many of my relationships don't work out — I'm probably lousy in bed. Not that I care one way or the other, which I'm sure is a big problem. But I don't really want to think about that. Anyway, I had black sheets. But not satin. I mean, have you ever lain down on satin sheets? They don't work. You slide off. Literally, you slide out of bed onto the floor. What good is that? The point of having a bed is you want to be in it, not on the floor. So the sheets were black, but not satin, and there was a picture of my favorite yogi on the wall because I was starting to get into that, and there were lots of candles, and all my favorite books on shelves. Then at the front of the apartment, right next to the door that opened onto the stairs, I had a little shelf and some stools set up, almost like a bar, so I could sit at my own little bar and look out the little cellar window through the grating at the pavement. The window was about a yard high off the pavement, so all I could see were people's feet. There were some flowers in front of the window, and I usually didn't have any lights on at night when I was sitting there. It was a great place to be a voyeur.

So what I used to do was play my music, and have a drink or a smoke, and work on being sad. Seriously. That's what I did. I would nurture the sadness, make it grow. I had this recording of Cole Porter's "Ev'ry Time We Say Goodbye" by Sarah Vaughn, which, for sure, was not jazz. She would sing it slower and slower each verse, and it got sadder and sadder until it was unbearable. I would also listen to the first movement of Rachmaninoff's Piano Concerto no. 3. I skipped the second and third movement because they were boring. It's a dark piece of music, which to me always seems to mean rainy days. Rainy days and sitting by my basement window looking at the feet, nurturing my pain. I really began to get into feet.

Have you ever looked at feet, and really thought about them? I'm not talking about some sick fetish; I'm talking about what feet say about people.

Well, I saw a lot of them, and they can be expressive. Some feet are happy, some feet are sad. Girls' feet are usually beautiful, and sexy, and cheery. I was nurturing my pain most during the summer so I saw a lot of open-toed slingback things. Very cheery. High heels are always heartbreaking. But they do look so elegant and special. In those days women used to wear a lot of them. And the guys' shoes? It really was more about trying to figure out what type of guy would buy those shoes. You could tell the really horrible guys — they had horrible shoes, pretentious and expensive, ridiculous most of the time. And then there were the real shoes. Sad shoes, the ones that showed a lot of wear and tear, and you could tell that the owner would like to buy new ones but he couldn't. You know what really broke my heart? The patched shoes. When somebody has to patch their shoes, then you know they're really poor. And on the girls, that's especially touching. Once I even saw a girl who was wearing patched shoes, little red high heels, and she had matching patched stockings. Women had to wear patched stockings during the war because stockings were scarce. But after the war, if a woman wore patched stockings you knew she was really just plain, old-fashioned poor. I wanted to run up there and hug the woman with the patched shoes and the patched stockings. But I didn't, I was too depressed.

So this dark, black depression thing went on and on. It got to a point where I figured that the only way I could get out of the depression was to get a real woman in my life, someone who would make me forget all about my main character.

It was then that I decided it was time to fall in love.

The best way to get an idea about what kind of guy I am is to think of a train station. When I'm trying to figure out if someone is a good person or not, I always apply the same test. What you do is you take a mental image of someone, and you put them in a train station. Then you ask yourself: if they were waiting for a train, what kind of a person would they be? You know, there's the old lady sitting all alone in the corner, dressed up to kill. She's probably taking the train to church. There are a couple of short-skirted sexy-type girls. Maybe they're wearing a little leather or something, hoping to meet up with some prince of a guy. There's the sensitive boy, sitting in the corner, reading a book. Then there's the ugly guy. There's always got to be an ugly one. Either the type who knows he's ugly — that's the more pitiful kind — or the type who doesn't have any idea. People stay away from him.

Actually, he smells, and doesn't know it, which is the most pitiful thing of all. Still, it's better not to know. Then there's the happy family, with Dad wearing some tacky vacation shirt, and Mom all dolled up for the trip, but a little frayed around the edges, the way mothers are. And the little boy is teasing the little girl, the way brothers always do. The little girl is wearing a pink cotton dress. There's a moderate amount of noise, in general. But you don't feel claustrophobic, because there's one of those big stone ceilings with the old fan way up high, circulating the air.

Then you spot me. I'm the guy sitting in the corner looking out the window. I don't want to look at anybody because I figure everybody's looking at me. They're probably not, but that doesn't really matter anyway. I'm wearing a trench coat, or maybe a full-length winter coat, depending on the season. But the point is, the collar is pulled up. That's essential, the pulled-up collar. And I'm sort of scrunched in the corner. I'd have my face pressed against the window if I could, but the window is too high above the bench to do that. I'm not bad-looking. Some people might even call me handsome. It's just that there's something about me, something that feels sort of hopeless. What I'm waiting for is my girlfriend to arrive on the next train. What I don't know is: she's going to break up with me.

Jesus Christ, there are a thousand reasons. Not that I smell or anything, but I can be pretty annoying. Bossy, self-centered, obsessed with my work. Not much fun actually. The kind of guy girls break up with all the time. But what's saddest of all is that, even though I know I'm probably worth breaking up with, and there is, in fact, every reason to break up with me, I don't expect it. No, not me.

Despite everything, I've still got hope.

I'm the guy sitting next to the window waiting for the train that's going to bring his girlfriend to town so she can break up with him and he doesn't know it. And he really should. But in this specific case, his stupidity is the nicest thing about him. Because everything he knows, he really knows. And everything he doesn't know, he really doesn't.

I'm that kind of guy.

So, it's up to you to decide whether or not to continue reading my story.

If you've ever read a newspaper or a literary magazine, you will come to the conclusion that I am a very famous person.

That's where you're wrong.

Let me explain. There is no such thing as a famous person. Famous people do not exist. Take Mary Tyler Moore for instance. Now, I have absolutely nothing against her. In fact, I worship at the altar of Mary Tyler Moore, in my own way. But she is not a person. I'm sure she tries to be a person, but that's not the same thing.

I'm not being completely clear. There may be someone called Mary Tyler Moore who looks like her and acts a little like her, and has the same voice, and who does the shopping, and whose son committed suicide, and who has diabetes. But Mary Tyler Moore is actually the woman whose name is in the papers, and people wonder about her failed marriage to Grant Tinker (how can they still remain friends?), and that younger psychiatrist guy she was seeing (did he psycho-analyze her into the sack?). And then, of course, there is Laura Petrie.

Laura Petrie.

Just saying the name sends shivers up my spine. It should send shivers up the spine of every right-thinking person. I know that's a severe thing to say, but it's the truth. Laura Petrie was actually called "Laurie" in the first few episodes. Take a look for yourself. You won't believe it, but Rob calls her "Laurie" and it sounds totally wrong. How could they think she was a "Laurie"? An infantilizing, cutesy name. She's obviously a "Laura." She has all the bewitching gauche-ness of Laura in the not-so-great Hollywood movie of the same name, starring Gene Tierney, who was not half as fas-cinating as Laura Petrie.

Laura with her foot stuck in the bathtub faucet, the way she sort of waves her hands around, rolls her eyes, and says, "Rob." When she cries, it's so pitiful. Not quite like the Lucille-Ball cry, which is more broadly comic, the Laura-Petrie cry has the ring of truth to it even though it's stretched in its own way. There are the skirts she wears, and how pretty she looks in them, there's her big teeth and her smile, and her dancing. At times she seems like an overgrown adolescent, which is perfectly fine, and at other times she is a wife and a seductress. She definitely tries her best and loves Rob very much even though he is a bumbling fool. And she's funny and smart. All these things are important.

Mary Tyler Moore is Laura Petrie. Even when she was on *The Mary Tyler Moore Show*, she was Laura Petrie.

The only way that you can escape fame, once it happens,

is to die in obscurity. This is not foolproof though, because people will still have imaginings about you. And those imaginings have power. If nothing else, fame is a testament to the power of the imagination.

I have tried to escape fame. Actually, let me make a larger and much more honest statement. I have tried to kill fame. I have hunted it down, stalked it the way a sportsman would a deer or an elk. But it has proved a wily foe.

The most lucid thing I can say about it is that fame doesn't exist. And yet it does. And of all the things in life you should be scared of, things that both exist and don't at the same time are the scariest. Ultimately, what I mean to say is that you have no idea who I am, even though you might think you do. I wish I could say it makes me laugh that you care who I am.

If you have to think I'm someone, then I suggest you think of me as being like the Unabomber. I live in a shack, even though it's a high-tech sort of shack, and I don't communicate with anyone in the outside world. And I write. So I might as well be him.

I might as well be anybody and nobody.

In fact, I am.

———

One of the problems is that you may think that I don't sound like a writer at all, that I sound ordinary. That's where you're both wrong and right. I am both an ordinary person and a writer, but most of all I don't believe in writerly writing. I don't believe in saying something in three words that could be said in two. I also don't believe in long or obscure words.

If you need a dictionary when you're reading, then you're reading a bad book.

It may seem that the lack of floweriness in my sentences means I have no concern for craft. This is not true. For me, the craft of a sentence does not always lie in its perfection, in a mathematical sense — but instead in its inspiration. Its rightness. If you have to analyze it, if you need exegesis, then it's all a dumb fraud. I guess James Joyce has some talent — at least he did before he started being a parody of himself — but *Ulysses* was a wrong turn for writing and for human beings in general. If you haven't read it, you're not missing anything. And if you have, and you think it's profound, then you're just a boring, pretentious person, and that's all there is to it.

I really don't want to get any into any arguments about this: you're not going to get any beautiful sentences here.

I am not Jesus Christ.

That probably seems obvious. When was the last time you picked up a book in a bookstore or library that happened to be by Jesus Christ? So obviously, I'm not. Or maybe it's not that obvious. The point is that I don't have the truth and I'm not blessed by any higher power. I seek enlightenment — a pompous word that sums up my religious beliefs — but I am not enlightened. I am imperfect, as all people are. So I don't want followers, should not have them. I don't want people quoting me, carrying my books in their pockets and doing crazy things. If they do, it's because they're crazy — not because of my books. I'm not trying to start a cult. Cults are

much, but whatever they paid them, they deserved more. The pleasure they gave us was worth more than any money you could ever have given them. Do you know what I mean?

So there I was, kind of hypnotized. I don't like quoting anybody, especially Hegel, so I'll paraphrase him. It was the way he described ballet — a plethora, an overabundance of thighs and calves and ankles, all waving at you. So good-naturedly too, there wasn't a lousy-looking or mean-looking girl in the bunch. I was kind of swaying, Manhattan in hand — I always have a Manhattan in Manhattan, I think it's only right — and this guy comes up to me. Or I guess I should say he starts sizing me up. He starts putting his hand in front of his eye like it's a viewfinder on a film camera or something, which always really makes me insecure. And then he says, "Don't I know you?" That's the starter, always the beginning of some hellish conversation. Gee whiz but I still to this day don't know what to say when people say that. I think the worst thing about these people is how masochistic they are, how they abuse themselves. It's sickening. "Hey, you don't know me, I don't matter. I'm nobody." For this reason I sometimes try to make the poor slobs tell me their names. Sometimes they refuse: "Oh listen, I'm not important." Jesus, what a way to go through life. And I'm not talking about a Zen thing here. Because the person doesn't really *not* care about themselves. In fact, the self-abuse is totally fake. They're completely self-obsessed and you're supposed to reassure them: "Don't say you're nobody. You're a person. Obviously, you're standing in front of me." Of course he asks me if I am The Famous Person. And I, because I hate lying, I tell him my name. Then he goes nuts. Now, I'm not taking any pleasure in this. Okay, to be perfectly honest, I am a tiny bit flattered when this happens, but that flattered feeling is so completely superseded by annoyance that it doesn't really count. Then, even though I'm the famous person and I'm revered, and next to God — according to this hellishly self-deprecating creep — what he's got to say about *himself* is much more important than anything I have to say. So he tells me all about how he's in advertising. What a surprise. He's retired now, but he used to write for television, and he's in town doing a benefit, and he's raised hundreds of thousands of dollars for some children's charity. Great. That's just great. I congratulate him, because I'm a nice guy. You might not believe it, but I am. And then he starts doing the other thing I despise, making all these cloying insulting links between the two of us. "We're both writers — I've always felt a connection with you, ever since we first met."

Apparently we met at some party in the even more distant past, which I find suspicious, since I hardly ever go to parties, but if it was ten years ago as he claims, I suppose it's possible. But this whole idea of a link between us is insane; it has no basis in fact. And he's drunk and his breath smells. Why do they always have bad breath? And then he says to the bartender, "Do you know who this is, do you know who you're serving at this bar?" And who cares whether the bartender knows. At this point, I'm so mortified. I'm watching the floor show with quiet desperation, just to block out the poison. Then he tells me about all the good that I've done in my life. Jesus, what does he know? And finally he says he's going to go home and write in his diary.

The reason I'm telling you this is because this man's sad

little soul is the soul of a critic. It is the soul of a person who has never done anything of any importance, or of value, who in fact has been sucked into the great American dream, but likes to imagine somewhere deep down inside that he's an "artist."

But he's not and he never will be. And nothing makes me madder than someone who pretends to be an artist. There are some people you just want to kill, but then you realize they're already dead.

So why bother?

When I decided to publish a story — an extended story in a series of stories, really — about a family with a particularly Jewish name, I got killed. Nobody liked it. One critic actually said that my writing about this family "represented the failure of the writer to understand his own true life experience and to fulfill himself." Jesus, that pissed me off. What right does some crapulent dolt have to speculate about whether or not I've fulfilled myself? That's for me and my God to decide, not some addle-brained dunderhead who scribbles garbage for the newspapers. Isn't it interesting, when I finally decided to be frank about my Jewishness — for myself, not for the damned critics, because I felt like it — I got completely massacred? Everyone else is deified for writing about their ethnic origins, but not me. I'm not necessarily saying it was a conspiracy, just that it was *interesting*.

What else?

I am not distanced enough from my characters. This leads

to the biggest criticism of all, the clincher — my real problem is that I *love* my characters too much. Yes, the critics say that, over and over: *he romanticizes characters, deifies them . . . as if he's in love with them.* What the hell's wrong with that?

Some people write offensive, irritating characters, other people create characters you wish were your best friends. Why is one necessarily better than the other? Some writers write out of love, others out of hate. Why is one a better impulse? Some want to build, others destroy. I don't think you can make a criticism based on the likeability of characters. You can say that they are not truly drawn, that no one would ever say those things, that they are not true to life. Because nice, smart, witty, good people exist in real life. Only rarely, however, do you get to meet one. So why not write about them? And why not write about potential? If it's interesting or inspiring to people, then what's the problem?

I'm criticized for writing like a kid. They say that I'm trying to ingratiate myself with college students by writing in the style of a kid, the way a teenager talks. As if this were intentional. I've always been young for my age, except when I was young. I was old then. I think that happens to a lot of people who don't have proper childhoods. I believe people need childhoods and adolescences. If they don't have them, they end up spending their lives trying to be young, to get back the years that they missed — years that were rightfully theirs. I have a kidlike way of communicating. I've always liked teenagers and kids more than adults. Only last week, my daughter said something to me about a hat I was wearing. I know I'm old now, but for some reason I decided to turn my cap around backwards the way the kids do. It was not about style. Who is going to see me out in the woods? It was because I was sitting outside, and the sun was hitting the back of my neck, and I was getting sunburned. My daughter thought this was very funny and said to her daughter, "Look, look, Grandpa's trying to be cool too!"

Jesus, I just turned my cap around.

Actually, I may be trying to reach kids. Young people, at least. It seems to me that they are the only ones worth reaching.

I just realized one reason I'm mentioning the critics: I was hurt by them. I'm surprised it didn't kill me, what happened with the critics. And you can think that I'm weak — I am. Or sensitive — I admit it. But it's really this: my work was conceived in innocence. Do you understand what that means? It means going inside yourself and pulling something out because you think it's important, like a rock or a diamond, or better yet the heart of an artichoke, except it's made out of the rarest crystal. You pull it out from inside you, from your very core, and you dare to show it to people. It's not for money, or for approval, or fame, or anything. It's just . . . showing. Like a kid at show-and-tell. Look, see this here? Isn't it pretty? And the goddamn teacher — because the critic is like a teacher — the teacher has the perfect right to say she doesn't like it, or to suggest improvements. But imagine a little kid brings a picture he drew of a cow on a farm to show-and-tell. The teacher not only tells him that it's badly drawn, but then impugns his motives: "Why are you trying to put one over on us? And why did you draw a cow like that? What have you got against cows? You're a sick kid, you know that? Sick. Sick for painting cows like that. Why are

you painting pictures of farms anyway? Have you got something against the city? Go sit down, and don't even think
about doing another drawing, you sick little freak."

This whole book is for that kid. And I just want to say,
"You go ahead. Keep drawing cows and farms if you want
to, if it makes you happy. It's not hurting anyone, it's okay. I
like your goddamn pictures. Call me crazy, but I do."

———

Another thing I get criticized for, and this really is ironic, is
hating people. So, on the one hand, they say I love my characters too much, that I'm too sentimental, and then they say
that the fact that I love the nice characters in my books too
much means that I'm uncharitable to other people, the bad,
boring people — to the world in general. I want to address
my "misanthropy" right now. A lot of this is related to the
fact that I have written positively about Buddhism, and especially the teachings of Sri Ramakrishna. His basic philosophy
is that you can spend your whole life looking for God in an
idol or up in heaven or in a book, but that God is in everything and is all around you. This I truly believe — not that it
matters what I believe. And because some critics have figured
that out, they have also decided that the way I raise some
characters over others is uncharitable. They figure that
because I'm a Buddhist I shouldn't be judgmental. First, I'm
not a yogi. I have not reached that stage of enlightenment and
I don't think I ever will. That's not an excuse, it's the truth.
More important, think for a minute, why am I so obsessed
with trying to love the world and forgive everyone? Because

that's my particular problem — because I'm such a misan-
thrope and hate people so much. I mean, it's why I hate cities.
I can barely walk down the street without wanting to kill
people. Have you ever noticed how people get in your way by
not looking where they're going? What about the people who
just stop and you bump into them because they were walking
in front of you? No explanation, no reason, they just thought
they'd stop, and, well — they're nuts. People are nuts. When
I used to take my kids to Radio City Music Hall I'd go crazy.
There'd be a great Hitchcock movie on or something and it
was important to expose them to all that joy, all that strangeness, all that precision. Because I'm sure they could learn
more from that than they'd ever learn from anything else in
their lives at the time. But sitting down in the audience?
People's conversations. I admit it. I'd have fantasies about
getting a gun and shooting everyone. I can't even explain it.
The stupidest things.

Some guy, let's say, abusing his girlfriend: "I told you to
take the beer out of the fridge before we left, so it would be
the right temperature when we got home."

"I'm sorry honey."

"Yeah, well, you don't have to drink cold beer."

"Yes, I do, I have to drink it too."

"Yeah but you don't care, because you're the one that
doesn't seem to mind drinking beer that's too cold."

"Most people like their beers cold, honey."

"Listen, I told you what I like, I like the beer cool but not
freezing, and if you had remembered to take it out of the
fridge, then it would be all right."

"I'm sorry. I'm sorry if I don't remember *everything*."

"You forget a lot of things."

"No, I don't."

"Yes, you do."

"Name one."

And it goes on and on. I want to rip my ears off — or rip his head off. What a sweet fellow. What a prince. Chews his girlfriend out in a crowded theater, in a loud voice, so everyone else can hear. Over his stupid beer. Over the right to get drunk on beer that's the right temperature. What, is he a cripple? He can't take his own beer out of the fridge himself? And what is she, his slave? I want to smash his face and run off with her. But then, if we got out of there, it would probably turn out that she was stupid too. Why would she hang out with the beer-drinking moron if she wasn't?

The point is that it's those faults, the ones you think will never go away because they are simply a part of who you are, it's those things you do your best to change. You may not succeed all the way. You may spend your life trying. So because I realize that my worst fault is misanthropy, I really do my best, I work on trying to be nice to people, on trying to understand them. It's true, I don't meet many people in the woods. But I do go down to the post office every day. And there's always someone there, picking up mail. Sometimes it's nice old Mrs. Smalley, and sometimes it's cranky old Mr. Dunt. Sometimes it's that woman who smiles too much, and is too fat, and is always swirling around in colorful print dresses that don't suit her, but might make sense on a woman half her age with a figure. I do my best not to kill these people. Just as I do my best not to kill my ex-wife. I guess I'm saying you should be thankful that I'm not a serial killer. Of course that sounds ridiculous, why would you be thankful for something like that? But you should be, take my word for it.

———

You may wonder if I was always like this. Slightly crazy. It got worse after the war. I was always like this, but before the war people would simply irritate me. After the war they'd make me want to shoot them. This suggests to me that the war took some things that were already inside of me and exaggerated them. It's not as if the war created some totally new trauma, it made what was already there much worse.

———

When I talk about my misanthropy, I mean my hatred for ordinary people, for the people that you meet at the store. Yes, the fact that I hate on a regular basis is a problem. The anger I feel towards my ex-wife, for example — that definitely has a pathological aspect to it, and it must be constantly confronted. Sure, when it comes to that stuff I'm totally nuts, I admit it. But when it comes to hating artistic people, literary people? When it comes to that, *I* am the sane one.

They still make me feel guilty, you know. When I do drag myself to some goddamn party because somebody is dying, someone I do really love — God people are horrible. I'm so glad I have nothing to do with them. I walk into a room and I can hear the buzz. And when people talk to me, it's always laced with venomous little "We never see you anymore" and "We've really missed you" type crap. Right, they missed me.

These are people who never, ever talked to me except to further their own stupid little careers. Of all the professions —
not that I have any real personal experience with the other
fields — the arts attract the worst class of people. By that I
mean the lazy liars, the unabashed hypocrites, the gossiping
guttersnipes. The worst of the worst. Let's face it, to be a
visual artist or a poet, or even a goddamn philosopher these
days, you don't have to actually learn anything, or know anything, or have talent. You can merely talk about what you do,
blather endlessly about the novel that you'll never write.

The people who go to those parties aren't writers at all.
They're not anything, not even people. Okay, sure, there are
a couple of real people there, like editors with actual taste,
but most are hangers-on, the art world is filled with them. I
do not have an ounce of guilt for deserting or hating these
people. That the history of art is made up of movements, of
people who hung out with each other and exchanged fabulous ideas, and wrote great things, almost communally, as a
group, is a myth. Garbage. No group of writers or artists ever
produced anything of any worth. Take the Bloomsbury
Group, for instance. Where's the fabulous list of writers and
artists from that group? Can't think of any besides Virginia
Woolf, can you? That's because she was the only fabulous
one. And she only had one or two really good friends, like
Lytton Strachey. I'm sure she had little time for the creeps
who hung around the old corner of Bloomsbury and Vine
pretending to be artists. Artists are loners for good reason:
you need to be alone if you are going to create anything sub-
stantial. People who hang around parties are not ever going
to produce art of any importance.

So when you go to one of these handy little shindigs, you're only going to meet people who have time to hang out at them, who are definitely not busy creating. You're going to meet the wannabes. And the wannabes are the first ones to sidle up to someone like me and make me feel guilty for not being around. As if I have deserted them. As if I have a duty or obligation. As if I owe it to them. But the thing is, they hate me. I make them uncomfortable. I actually have ideas, have opinions, and think. I'm real. Sure, these people are so busy pleasing other people, and making up nice things to say to further the careers they will never have, that no negative energy comes from them. On the surface they seem quite nice. In contrast, I know I appear strange. So tall and thin and dark and menacing. Can I help it if God gave me a long face? I don't have to *pull* a long face, I just *have one*. So stop accusing me of being dark, and gruesome, and not smiling. When I smile these days, I look like a grinning skeleton. You don't want to see it. Really, you don't.

You know when I stopped going out in public? When people started accusing me of becoming a hermit for effect. No, seriously, I couldn't believe it myself. Some damn critic — who else? — wrote that the reason I had holed up in the woods, and refused to speak to anybody except the people at the post office, was because this kind of activity made me more mysterious. In other words, becoming a hermit was a bid for attention. After all, you make yourself inaccessible, won't people want to try to find you? Have you ever heard of anything so ridiculous? I don't hide in the woods in order to get more attention. I hide in the woods because I'm a dangerous man. Dangerous to myself, and to others. I think I would take a sledgehammer to people if I had to be around them. And, the woods is, simply, the best place for me to write.

———

Even if it's not pleasant for you to read about all the ways in which I am selfish, and hateful, and inadequate, it's good for me to write them down. At other times this all might seem like self-justification. If I appear to be defending myself, it's because I'm angry about an untruth. Untruths are like weeds that must be pulled before they can ruin the rest of the garden.

This brings me to the worst review I've ever received. To words I almost can't stand to write. This means that they're very important. The more painful, the more necessary. One reviewer, who shall remain nameless — except to say that his name sounds a lot like "letch," which is more than a coincidence in this case — when discussing one of the more famous relationships in one of my more famous books, actually suggested that the main character had more than just a loving relationship with his younger sister. He insinuated that the character was in some way sexually interested in a little girl. Now, this wouldn't be so bad except for two things. First, the reviewer didn't come out and say this outright because, coward that he is, he was completely aware that his allegations were false, and therefore he wanted to give himself an out. *I didn't really say that, you inferred it.* Second, he implied I did not purposely set out to write about an incestuous relationship or the evils of molestation, but in fact had inadvertently written about the subject because I am a pederast.

The dirty, cowardly, evil insinuation didn't stop there. What this letch described was taken up and faithfully implied by several other reviewers, to the point that my novels, and most of my writing, are now considered suspect. Naturally, this made me very angry and very sad, more angry and sad than you can imagine. Not because I care for anything as stupid as my "reputation," but because I couldn't believe the depths to which people would sink, out of jealousy, to discredit my work. It goes on and on. My first novel always got a bad rap for leading youth astray. Which it didn't. If anything, it helped them, I'm sure of it. But because my first novel also happened to be found in the pockets of several famous persons, particularly one or two assassins, or would-be assassins, I now have a reputation for writing evil books, books that lead people to do bad things.

By cutting myself off from a media-hungry, publicity-crazy world, what has happened is that I have succeeded, completely by accident, in increasing the malignant speculation about both my private life and my motives.

By the time you read this I'll be dead, and it will be time for the truth. Not that I'm without faults, but the specific neurotic little circumstances of my life don't happen to include child molestation or the creation of evil. Anyone who reads my writing and has half a brain understands that my work is exactly the opposite. Because I am innocent. Or, at least, I started out that way. The tragedy of life is that it's almost impossible to remain innocent. What I want to do here is tell you about my innocence, and about how it was gradually taken away. About the war.

But I'll start with the other betrayals, the later betrayals, the more minor betrayals. Because there are still certain things that I can't write about. Not yet.

Just a quick style note. (You might not think I'm paying attention to style, but I am.) I know it seems weird — and it will become even weirder — that I don't refer to anyone by their actual names, including myself. (I go on about "my daughter" or "critics" anonymously, but when it comes to the women in my life, I've changed their names — to protect the innocent.) Also, I'm not going to quote from my books. In a way this doesn't make sense, I know. It's not as if you can't figure out who I am. But all this is related to the way my brain works. I need the illusion of privacy. Which brings me to why I would even write this. It's the kind of book I should never have written, that I promised never to write. But certain incidents — horrible, nightmarish incidents — have forced my hand. And also, if I were to use real names, it wouldn't seem like fiction. Sure, it's all true, but it's important for me not to *think* it's true. The best type of writing is when the author is trying to fool himself that what he is writing is a lie.

I have to clear up one other thing. It's about the flit in my most famous book. The main character — the one I took so much time saying goodbye to — becomes disillusioned because, in the end, an older man comes on to him. So, some critics have accused me of having something against queers. I don't have anything against queers. I'm not going to say that some of my best friends are queers. I don't think my best friends are queers, but then again, I don't even know or care what most people do in bed. Some of the guys at the *New Yorker* might be queers, I think. I'm not sure. Anyway, I didn't *mean* to suggest by this passage in the book that queers are bad people. I'm sure there are nice queers out there. This particular queer, though, was abusing his position as a teacher by coming on to a teenage boy. The boy felt betrayed, not because the man was queer and came on to him, but because he was his teacher, and a queer, and came on to him. It's no problem if somebody wants to be a fag and do fag things, but it's a big problem if a teacher comes on to a student. I'd feel the same way about a male teacher and a female student.

I don't know how people could be so stupid as to think I was against queers because I wrote about this fag in a negative way. Actually, I do. People are stupid. That's a fact.

———

So, 1951. The black apartment. The black sheets.

I probably should have gotten a cat. But I didn't, because I realized I was in danger of becoming a really sad person. It's still a danger today, actually, because I think really sad people think they can do without other people. Sometimes I think I can do without them, and then I realize that's impossible, so I have to fall in love. Being in love isn't really like being with other people.

You'll probably think I'm overly romantic. I suppose that might be a bad thing, but I refuse to think it is. Maybe it is impractical. Psychiatrists go on and on these days about how you're not supposed to model your ideas of love on romantic movies. But the truth is that I still believe the movie stuff. The old ones. Nowadays they don't tell you anything. So maybe that means I'm permanently screwed up. I guess that's a distinct possibility. Anyway, the movie that says it all for me is *Now, Voyager*. First of all, there's Bette Davis's whole transformation from an unbelievable one-eyebrowed geek who smokes in secret to this incredibly glamorous thing in hats. That's worth the price of admission. And of course, Bette Davis is completely believable in the role because she's not, essentially, pretty, and you can tell she knows she's not — Bette Davis, as well as the character. Bette Davis's own book is called *The Lonely Life* — aptly enough — and it really is good as celebrity autobiographies go. It's easy to tell Bette is the type of gal who has to be told she's beautiful. They're the best. The ones who absolutely know they are beautiful can get boring. The Davis-types are the girls I look for, anyway. I'm sure any smart guy will tell you this: that the ones who don't know they're cute are incredibly sexy, like diamonds in the rough, like flowers that open up just for you — and I don't mean that in a gross way. Never mind the fact that there's something humble and sweet about not knowing you're attractive. I'm sure this makes me sound selfish and insecure. But if you think about it, it makes sense. There's something about helping a person realize she's beautiful and special that magnifies the whole love experience.

But Bette learning to love herself isn't the best part of the movie. It's the love she discovers in South America — Jerry. Not that he's anything to write home about in the looks department — too suave and mustachioed — but that's really the point. What she loves about Jerry — besides the fact that he makes her realize that she's really a woman — is that they can laugh together. They have crazy, silly fun. They almost get into a car accident, but turn it into romance. They share an adventure: love blossoms. Jerry is already married, of course — that's the obstacle. They have to part; naturally, her psychiatrist recommends she marry a boring banker. I can't actually remember if he's a banker, but he's a banker sort of person. Now it's great the way the psychiatrist helps her rebel against her mother, but I've got to disagree with the banker recommendation. It's typical of why I hate psychiatrists, really. Settle, oh just settle — grow up and have a calm life, go for the safe choice, it'll be better in the end. Right. You'll be more mentally balanced. Forget about Jerry, have a lobotomy, take a pill. Even the banker is better looking than Jerry — in an old, distinguished, banker sort of way — but he's not fun. Or dangerous. That's the main thing about love, or one of the main things: that it's dangerous, that you always think you're going to fall off that cliff — whatever the cliff may be.

Whatever you do, don't settle for the banker.

She doesn't, thank God. Then just when she thinks she is going to spend the rest of her life as a glamorous, elegant, poised, fashionable, lonely spinster — only in the movies — the girl who is staying at the sanatorium with her turns out to be Jerry's daughter. Coincidence of coincidences! This is where the flick gets kind of mawkish but still stays true. Bette Davis decides to help Jerry's daughter so she can be friends with Jerry. Then the final line: "Why ask for the moon, when we have the stars!"

Good question. But I'll take the moon *and* the stars if I can. Of course, at that time you couldn't make a movie about a woman who ends up sleeping with a married man and have them live happily ever after. But the reason she says she has the stars with Jerry — even though they're not doing the nasty — is because Jerry is a lot of fun to be with, romantic and dangerous, so she takes whatever she can get.

That might sound masochistic, but it's not. The reason is, well, it's all related to that song from *South Pacific*: "Some Enchanted Evening." There's a line, "Once you have found her, never let her go." It's important. When you find that person who makes you laugh, who really makes you laugh, with no faking, then that's the person you should be with. This is what I mean when I say that I'm a crazy romantic. It's the most difficult thing in the world, finding a kindred spirit, someone who really understands you — the movies you like, the way you think, the way you feel about the world. And when you find that person, it's almost as if you don't have to talk, you just have to look at them. But you do end up talking, because talking is the best part.

So when I knew that the book was going to be over, and that my best friend — the main character — was going away forever, I knew the only thing I could do was find a new best friend. If I wasn't going to go crazy, I had to fall in love.

Do you know what it's like to be looking for love? I don't mean desperately, of course. I don't mean that malignant feeling where you don't have any self-esteem and you'll settle for anybody — that never works. I mean when you are completely calm inside, because you feel incredibly good about yourself. You also feel that you could make it on your own. It's only then that love — true love — comes. When you have that feeling, you're kind of blessed. There's a glow about you. Please understand, there's a difference between being a lonely screwed-up guy in a black apartment, who stares at people's feet and is going to die if he doesn't get lucky, and somebody who lives in an all-black apartment, stares at people's feet, and knows that there is a hole inside of him that only a beautiful girl can make right. It doesn't mean that he's going to kill himself if he doesn't get her. After all, he's made it on his own before. He made it through the war, and what came after. But he's very centered, and coasting around town with an open heart.

This was me, and it explains why I finally made it out of the house. I knew I couldn't go to any stupid jazz clubs — the smugness would kill me — so I had to go to parties.

God, I hate parties. But you already know that, right?

For someone like me a party is Chinese water torture. I don't want to sound puritanical, especially about language, but words are too important to throw around. And that's what people do at parties, they just throw them around. I guess it's partially because — no matter how centered I was, and how focused I was on looking for the perfect girl in a completely Zen way — I got myself into some pretty horrible situations before finding what seemed like a good match.

For instance? Once, my sister had a friend who was having a party. She knew I was depressed, and invited me. The plan was created to help me combat my mother's notion that I should move back home. I was almost thirty years old and I wasn't going to move back in with my mother, no matter how depressing everybody thought my apartment was. My sister knew about my apartment. I brought her there once — once was enough. I think it really sent her into a tail-spin. She figured that I was going to do myself in there, and she made it her mission to get me invited to a stupid party to cheer me up — not that she'd ever say anything bad about my apartment — but I could tell the way she stumbled over her words when she told me how much she liked it.

You'd really like my sister; she's not a bad person. I think what I like most is her hope — she really does try to discover the best in people. She's kind of the opposite of me in that way. In fact, in every way. But opposites attract I guess, and I admire her courage, even though I think it's totally hopeless. Her hope, I mean. My sister is the kind of person who likes doilies, and carousels, and holidays. Don't get me started about holidays. Let's just say that holidays are all about false-ness, and trying to love people that you don't really love at all — people God saddled you with as a stupid joke. But not for my sister. They are the center of her life. I'm not trying to be-little her. I really admire people who are opposite to me, especially when they are good at things I'm not. My sister is the type who would start crying at her birthday dinner and say, "You ruined my birthday," as if a birthday wasn't already ruined by being another birthday. And you'd think I'd despise her for it, but I don't. She's got such a hopeless life. Her hus-band was a sweet guy, but he died suddenly of a heart attack and left her with nothing. She breaks her back working at Bloomingdale's. Imagine, dealing with those bargain-crazed old ladies every day. For a while she did secretarial work at night. At night, if you can believe it. She's also partially blind, and has to wear thick glasses. But she's never complained — except when her birthday's ruined — and she's always managed to look on the bright side. She has to, with so much going badly for her. Actually, she's got at least ten different diseases, but it doesn't matter. I simply love her. Osteoporosis will probably put her in a wheelchair someday, but rainbows and daisies will always cheer her up. And she's smart, she really is. Take my word for it.

So she was going on and on about how lovely my apartment is, but should I be sitting in it all the time and watching people's feet? It wasn't so much that I thought she had a point, as I thought I'm ready. I'm ready for the love thing.

The party is in some little old house in Queens, and this friend of hers is another lady who works at Bloomingdale's. She's another cheery one. Cheery in a dumb way, not heroic at all. It's a tiny house, old-fashioned, and, I suppose, charming. When I get there, about seven o'clock at night, it's cocktails — it's summer and it's still light. I can see through the dining-room picture window right away that she has a beautiful garden, and I think: why wouldn't she hold the party out there? This is one of my big problems. I get an idea like that in my head and it makes me so angry I could scream or bash something. Here are all these people stuck in a hot little house, which isn't even charming, and all she'd have to do is open the door, let us out in the backyard, and we might have a swell time. But she doesn't, and that makes me cranky as hell. Almost everyone is the shopgirl type — nothing against shopgirls, except I don't have much to say to them. And her friend Gloria's husband's old Ukrainian grandmother is sitting in the corner looking disapproving. People like that always get on my nerves. I know I should ignore them, and their disapproval, but it's impossible. I can't. I get obsessed with the one person in the room who is really mean and nasty, and can't stop imagining what's going on in their head. Like this old woman: all I could think about was how unhappy she was, being in the United States — she was wearing a babushka — and how much happier she'd be back in the old country. And how she was going to die here all alone — even though she was with her family — so far away from quaint Ukrainian folk dances, and other homegrown customs.

Jesus, what do you do in these situations? I stand around shuffling my feet and staring into my cocktail worrying about everybody. God, I wish sometimes I wasn't so tall. I take up so much room, and I always feel obligated to talk to people to justify the space. So there I was chatting up some shopgirl — to justify being there and please my sister — about what a bargain it was to buy stuff at Bloomingdale's and through the door walked this vision. I remember she was wearing something feathery and light with lace. Chiffon? Whatever, it was tasteful — a sheer fabric that still covered her decently in all the right places. She was also wearing a beautiful, airy shawl. I noticed right away that she had strong legs, but there was something in the way she moved (to quote a Beatles song, inadvertently) that was still so incredibly graceful and unself-conscious. She was completely unaware of how perfect she was. Every way that she moved or looked was poised, special, but she wasn't trying to be that way, she just was. She reminded me of an animal — a deer would be too paranoid, a panther too predatory; something in between. I couldn't take my eyes off her.

Unfortunately she was with someone who cornered the market on creepiness. It is always beyond my *comprehension* how girls like her end up with guys like him. I guess there aren't too many fascinating guys around. But why can't perfect girls hook up with someone who is merely boring and banal? Why the arch prince of boorishness?

This guy was wearing a tailored suit, which I guess he looked spiffy in, making me feel very stupid in my sports jacket. His suit was a little too tailored if you asked me, almost Mafioso style. I've got nothing against wearing clothes that fit, but you can take these things too far. I suppose he had a good body, if you are into that sort of thing.

But Jesus, the crap that spewed from his mouth. I could hear every word, the whole party could — they could probably hear him in Manhattan — because as soon as he came in he started talking very loudly. You know the type of person who wants everyone to hear what they're saying? It's a performance. Except no one is actually entertained. From the moment that I heard him speak, I could tell that nothing but garbage was going to come from him. Turned out that he was a manager at Bloomingdale's, big Jesus deal, and television people were coming in to film a commercial. He kept talking about "television people" as if they were a new species of elk or something. "*Television people* are so wonderful. It's great dealing with them, they're so polite, so professional." As if he knew anything about professionalism, but he sure wanted the whole room to think he did. Jesus, he made me want to take a crap on the rug right there, which, I know, is an awful thing to say, but you get the idea.

Anyway, there came a point in the party when somebody decided to put on a record with some English twit singing a song called "Have Some Madeira, M'Dear!" Now, normally, I would have nothing against this sort of thing, most English comedy songs are quite funny. But there's something about this one that gives me the willies. I think it's the fact that only boring people play it, and when they get to the part of the song where the guy says, "Have some Madeira, my deah!" everybody sings along, which is enough to make me psycho. I knew that if I stayed in the room, I was going to have to sing that stupid, horrible song, and all I could think about was how much fun that girl's Mafioso boyfriend would have singing it too. So I couldn't stay there, I had to go to the kitchen and get some ice. It was a quaint little kitchen that also had a view of the garden, and I could hardly hear "Have Some Madeira, M'Dear!" which goes to show you they sure don't make houses the way they used to. And of course, coincidence of coincidences — but it wasn't — in sailed the vision. I knew she was pissed off about the song. She looked irritated, and, as much as I wished it were caused by her companion, I could tell it was the song.

For once in my life I said the right thing at the right time. "Not big on sing-alongs?"

"No," she said. Only slightly tired, and not the least bit sarcastic. I respected that. She could have said, "Not really," which would have turned me off, or said, "No, sirree," and laughed like a donkey. But she said, "No," very simply, and walked to the window over the sink. That meant she had to lean on the sink, and the early evening light hit her dress, and I had to keep from narrowing my eyes to test how sheer it really was. God, she looked gorgeous. And she just stayed there, looking out the window — with absolutely no idea of how incredibly gorgeous she was, I swear.

"It's a beautiful garden," I said.

"Yes," she said. It was all so relaxed and natural. My comment had made her study the garden, and now she was enjoying it, right in front of me. She was completely lost in the moment. I really admire people who can get lost in the moment. It's something I have a hard time doing, but it's an important spiritual talent. Most people live in the past or the future, few live in the present. If you meet someone who lives in the present, then you've met a very spiritual person. We talked a little bit about the flowers and the birds. I was essentially ignorant about gardens. I told her I had a little patch of land in front of my black apartment that I didn't do anything with, but that some pretty flowers had grown there. We even talked a little bit about some Buddhist ideas — that is, the idea of not planning things, just letting them happen. At some point it came up that she was a dancer, which made perfect sense to me — she obviously wasn't a shopgirl. Then just when things were going great, in came The Big Tycoon himself, the Bloomingdale's manager who told her to come into the living room and join the fun — he was going to sing some old college songs to the shopgirls in the other room. It was completely typical; he would be into college songs, love showing off that he went to college. The poor shopgirls would be so impressed. It was so sad.

I couldn't stand it any longer so I did a crazy thing.

I invited them both back to my apartment for a drink.

It was a completely mad thing to do. And rude to the

party at large, removing two of the only young men there —
out of reach of all those needy shopgirls. Worse, I wasn't the
least bit interested in having *him* at my apartment, just her.
He was such a fathead that I knew he wouldn't know that I
didn't want him there — he probably thought I wanted a job
at Bloomingdale's. In fact, in the cab back to Manhattan, he
asked what I did for a living. I said I was a writer. He gave
me his business card and said that a job might come up. It
was stupid of me to invite two people back to my apartment
when all I wanted was to make out with the girl, which
would only happen if I were to murder the goof who was
with her. I knew she would come back to my place because
she was a free spirit, completely in tune with the mood of the
moment. And he thought it was a big deal that I lived in
Greenwich Village, because, as he said, "It's so bohemian."
He kept asking me if it was true that only freaks lived there.
I said, "I live there, don't I?" He looked at me like I was
going to kiss him or something, which was definitely opposite to the feeling I had at the time.

I don't think he'd ever seen anything like my black apartment before. I actually think he imagined I was into devil
worship. He kept asking me, "Do you do some sort of ritual
here?" It was embarrassing. Yeah, sure, I performed rituals,
I'm a religious person. But I know that's not what he meant.
He meant some sort of cultish thing where you sacrifice goats
or molest children. That was the kind of guy he was, and the
kind of garbage that was rotting his brain.

The girl — her name was Andrea — was walking around
my apartment, looking at all my books, while he and I were
sitting in the living room having drinks. It looked like I was

going to end up spending the night talking to *him*. Then she found my Sri Ramakrishna. The book immediately sparked her interest. I couldn't believe that she had such a poised and organic Buddhist energy, and then, on top of it all, she picked out the most important book, the *only* important book in my apartment — even with Kafka, Flaubert, and Chekhov staring her right in the face.

"What's this?" she asked.

And when I told her it was a book about Zen Buddhism, she told me that she had heard of it, which, again, I found almost impossible to believe. But considering her energy, it made perfect sense in every way.

"Can you explain it to me? Or is that impossible?"

I thought the two alternatives showed enormous sensitivity. So I told her that maybe this wasn't the time or the place. I was awkwardly and obviously hinting at the possibility of a date. Then I got the great idea to use my window to tell her.

I said that if we went over to the window, we could do a very Zen thing — look at people's feet. I explained how doing that was like Buddhism, because it would be enjoying the "now."

Then I made the mistake of talking about how God might be in some poor slob's feet.

It was at this point that Mr. Bloomingdale's began to lose it. Maybe Andrea believed that it was me who cracked. I still think it was the manager guy.

"What did you say? God is in feet?"

"God is everywhere," I said.

"But did you say it's in people's feet?"

"That's one place you find it."

"You can't find God in people's feet."

"As I say, that's just an example of the many places where you can —"

"We're getting out of here. Come on, Andrea, we're going."

"What's the problem?"

"I said we're going, bud. We've got your number."

"What are you talking about?"

"You know what I'm talking about."

"No, I don't."

"We're not into this perverted foot stuff either."

"What perverted foot stuff?"

"Look, I'm not going to spell it out for you."

It went on like this for a minute or two. I asked Andrea if she wanted to stay, but she didn't know what the problem was, so Mr. Bloomingdale's had to spell it out. He assumed I was a foot fetishist and that was it for me. So I had to explain to him that I was into shoes, not feet, and what shoes said about a person. So he said, "Oh, right, shoes. I believe that, buddy." That set me off, and I started yelling about how evil the mind is, and how this is what's wrong with everybody — the world is benign, it's just waiting for us to experience it, but half the time we can't do that because some half-wit is going to tell us that it's perverted, and it's because the perversion is in his head, and he should seriously take a look at his head, because he's looking at the world through perverted eyes.

Of course she left with him. I could tell she understood exactly what I was saying, even though she seemed kind of scared of me. But I had reason on my side, I was making sense, and I know she knew it, no matter what my sister thought. You see, my sister said afterwards that Andrea thought I was a bit crazy. I guess she didn't say "a bit," she said "crazy." And obsessed. I still find that hard to believe. I know that somewhere deep inside of Andrea she knew that it was okay to look at people's feet — their shoes really — and that I was doing it for all the right reasons.

Afterwards I tried to forgive her. I told myself she came to the party with the creep, and any girl who goes to a party with one guy and leaves with another one, no matter how creepy the first guy is, deserves to be tried in the court of romance, if one exists somewhere. If one doesn't, believe me, it should. But I still blamed myself. And all the horrible thoughts came back.

I haven't really told you about them.

Sometimes I have horrible thoughts about the whole notion that I am crazy. I think it's related to the fact that I spend so much time alone and getting into my own head. But especially after an incident like this — opening up my heart and starting to talk about something important, like people's feet, only to be treated like a creature from another planet — I begin to think that maybe they're right and I am crazy. My sensitivity can definitely get out of hand. I have so little tolerance for stupidity, or, worse, boringness. Sometimes I think I have what they now call ADD, only I don't have trouble concentrating, I just need to be stimulated all the time or I go nuts. I need to have new ideas to engage, and beautiful things to think, and funny things to laugh at. That's why I like old movies, because they give you all this stuff. And it's why I like falling in love, because, for a while at least, I'm away from my own mind — a mind that can sometimes eat itself alive. People have always told me: "Get some interests, get a hobby." Jesus Christ, if anybody ever tells me to get a hobby again, I think I'll kill them. People like me don't have hobbies. Hobbies are for people who have boring jobs, who don't love what they do. I love writing, it's the only thing I love, and the only thing that keeps me sane. And I don't have to escape from it, I have to do it more, it's the only way I can get a perspective on things.

Except around this time, if you remember, I didn't have anything to write because I had just said goodbye to the most wonderful friend I'd ever had. So the only thing to do was to fall in love. The whole Andrea thing hadn't worked out, I told myself, because she was perfect in every way except one: she had fallen for a creep who had obviously brainwashed her. It can happen to the best of us. My mistake was in believing that because she lived in the moment and seemed very Zen she was perfect in every way. Obviously, she was not. And I wasn't crazy. Jesus, what was I doing believing the opinion of some guy who was the manager of a bargain basement, and impressed by people in television? Looking back on it all now, sometimes I don't believe myself, I really don't.

The argument with the Bloomingdale's manager had been pretty terrifying, but I knew if I stewed on things like this I'd do something even crazier. That's why I accepted an invitation to a *New Yorker* party — which was crazy in itself.

I won't go on about my whole *New Yorker* thing now. I really don't know why it was such a big deal for me. The obsession was part of the worldly stuff I was trying to get rid of at the time. Let's face it, one reason I try so hard to rid myself of worldly passions — and desires, and ambitions — and just live in the moment, and look at people's feet, is because I've been disappointed by the world. I'm sure you've figured that out. In fact, that's a good thing. That's what Buddhism teaches you. The world is a disappointing place. Desire is a streetcar — the whole thing is a streetcar — and the sooner you step off it and smell the roses the better. So, yes, I completely separated myself from the *New Yorker* because of how they had treated me. It's all egotism, and it shouldn't matter, but what can I say, I'm human. It hurt. I had, stupidly, asked the *New Yorker*, through my agent, to publish excerpts from my novel before it appeared. You know, the one with the character I was having so much trouble saying goodbye to. They refused, citing two reasons. Both incredibly stupid and insulting.

They said that the family in my book was too precocious — that no living family could ever be that fabulous. Now I want you to think about that for a minute. Could anything be stupider? Have you ever met any precocious families? If you haven't met any, have you ever heard of any? I'm sure there are whole families of nuclear physicists somewhere, and if someone decides to write about them, then more power to them. As I said before, why should it be better to write about non-brilliant, mean people than brilliant, kind people? So we can throw that criticism right in the garbage. But it was their second criticism that really bugged me. They said that the reason they didn't like the novel was because I was obviously too wrapped up in it, that I was "imprisoned" by its mood.

At least they got that partly right. Yes, I was imprisoned by the novel's mood, that's for sure, that's why I was living in a black apartment in Greenwich Village and having arguments with fathead managers from Bloomingdale's. But can you tell me what writer worth his or her salt isn't totally "imprisoned" by what they write? Isn't that the point of writing, to be imprisoned, to be lost in it so that other people can get lost in it too? I think what I hate most is being criticized for things that are actually virtues. Being criticized because I do something right. It's all part of that whole thing about me loving my characters too much. But if you're a stupid, obnoxious editor without a brain in your head that's what you'd think.

The subject of editors brings up something else *New Yorker*-related. One of my favorite editor friends was seriously ill. At the time we weren't sure with what, but naturally it turned out to be cancer. This makes perfect sense to me now — he smoked like a fiend. But also, he was a perfect person. Or at least a perfect editor and a really nice person. It always seems to me that perfect people die young. That's one of the horrible things about the world, but you have to get used to it. I don't really know how to describe him. Let's just say that he was a gentle soul in a sea of vipers, someone who floated through the literary miasma with a grace and wit that was nonpareil. I know I said I don't like big words, but he deserves them. Not that he was a particularly graceful person. He was short, and fat, and not very attractive. But he was intelligent, and calm, and sweet. The most important trait in an editor is to have no ego. So what happens? The opposite kind of person is attracted to the job — those who can't, teach. Editors, like critics, are almost always sad

bouncy, which was appealing when she was young. This was, however, beginning to wear thin — because she didn't have anything left to bounce. But it was still sort of sweet, all that positive energy, even though sometimes she could be a bit too enthusiastic.

So it would be bearable, and they had a beautiful apartment, as New York apartments go, and by that I don't mean sparse and no furniture, but crammed to the gills with books and knick-knacks, real things that they loved. I knew the party would be filled with the wrong kind of editors and people asking me about my book, which was about to be — I guess I forgot to tell you — published. This fact was something I was trying to distance myself from. On one hand, people would be able to read it and get to know the guy who had been my best friend for so many years — that was nice, in a way, I guess. On the other, I was jealous, because people were going to get to meet the guy for the first time, when I was going through the trauma of saying goodbye. And they would be saying things like, "Aren't you thrilled?" when actually, no, I wasn't. I was terminally depressed, almost suicidal. It's hard to tell people that; they think you're not being a good sport. They don't understand, because they think a novel is all about having people read it and getting good reviews, when actually a novel is all about the writing. When it's published, the best part is over.

I always remember a comment Hitchcock made to some actor — Robert Taylor I think — who one day asked him what he was thinking. That's a problem in itself of course. No one should ever ask anyone what they are thinking. People have been killed for less, as far as I'm concerned. It's not fair to try to wedge your way into someone else's brain. If they want to tell you, they will. If they don't, it's for a good reason. But ol' Hitch was surprisingly nice to this stupid, prying actor and said, "I'm thinking about my next movie." And then he explained — laboriously I'm sure — that the fun for him was in *conceptualizing* the film, that the actual *making* of it was boring. That's because he was a real creator, not some hack who got off on applause and attention.

Oh yeah, there was another thing I had to contend with (speaking of Hollywood): one of my short stories had just been made into a movie. I wouldn't tell you about this at all except to give you an idea of the pressure I was under. I mean, I can't even stand to think about that movie. They took one idea from my story, the situation really, and chopped out everything else to make a mawkish, sentimental piece of garbage. I'm still upset. Not about my name being in the credits — I couldn't care less about that — but about simply being a part of such an evil thing. Enough about Hollywood. I don't know how Hitchcock survived it. He deserves twenty-five Academy Awards for maintaining his integrity. As far as I'm concerned, Hollywood kills writers. F. Scott Fitzgerald wrote tons of movies, though not many were actually produced. But he worked his ass off, then drank himself to death out of depression over the thick-headed lack of response to his genius. It's a crime what Hollywood does to people.

So I guess it won't seem strange that I was hiding in a corner at this shindig. That was the nice thing about that particular apartment. It was one of those railway setups — incredibly long. Those apartments are badly made from a privacy point of view — which is a major concern for me about any living space. A railway apartment, though endlessly long, is made up of, let's say, ten rooms, all of which open onto each other in a straight line. You have to go through one room to get to another. So if your bedroom is the last room, for instance, well, you'll have to walk through every other room to get to the kitchen, which is often at the front. But they're still very charming. At the time I remember thinking that this couple must have really been in love to live so intimately; it would have driven me crazy. Anyway, to make more space, The Literary Couple had opened up every room in the apartment, and I, smart guy that I am, had managed to wend my way through hundreds of horrible people without talking to them, installing myself in the back bedroom in a corner between two bookcases. Only essentially good people have bookcases filled to the brim in their *bedrooms*.

The wife writer had promised to get me a drink, and sure enough she did, so I made certain she talked to me and kept me busy. This was the perfect spot in the apartment and I was lucky to get it. No one could see me unless I wanted them to, but I could get a pretty good view straight through every room to the front, if I wanted to, by craning my neck. The wife writer had started to irritate me a bit — perhaps I should say worry me — but I thought I was safest with her. At least she was smart and eternally bubbly. What was worrying was that she was going on about some new young talent she had discovered, or claimed she had discovered. She was calling him a "young Saroyan." Not that I've got anything against Saroyan — actually he's one of the few American writers I admire. But there's no such thing as a "young Saroyan." First of all, it's not Saroyan's fault that he's old, or older than some other guy, and second, if the writer is any good at all he's not a young anything, he's just himself. Also, it seemed to me that this woman was kind of collecting young writers and getting overly excited about too many of them. She actually had discovered a couple of talented people — including me — but I was beginning to suspect her motives. I can respect someone who is in awe of talent, but is that what was really going on? Or was it about showing off and attaching herself to the hot thing of the moment?

I had another concern of a personal, romantic nature. She kept talking about how cute and sweet this guy was, referring to a lock of hair that fell over his eyes. All I could think was, he sure does sound more attractive to you than your husband. Was it possible the woman was contemplating an affair? She had never tried to seduce me, thank God, but the idea that she was not only collecting young writers but trying to get them into bed was nauseating. And then I began to wonder — I wonder too much for my own good sometimes — thinking of her short, fat, brilliant, weary husband, if they had some sort of arrangement. That kind of thing always makes me upset. People can do anything they want to as far as I'm concerned — but don't be New York's perfect literary couple and then have sex with other people. Or worse yet, maybe he was a flit — and they were both going to have sex with the guy. This would be the ultimate horrification. Not, again, that I have anything against flits. It would just be so . . . dishonest.

So it was as these thoughts were running through my brain — just as I was starting to not have a very good time, and be suspicious of the only people at the party that I thought were nice at all — that it happened.

I saw her.

I was going to write, "There she was," but Virginia Woolf already used that at the end of *Mrs. Dalloway*.

Because I was getting so upset with the wife writer, I craned to look down the railway line to see how many horrible people I might have to avoid saying hello to on my way out. And then I saw this girl standing at the other end of the apartment. Or I guess I should say she was standing at the edge of the kitchen, on her way into the living room — literally on the threshold. The kitchen was dark to make it more like a party room, and there was an otherworldly table light right by the archway into the living room, and it lit her up as if she was unreal.

But she was very real.

I hope you won't take it the wrong way if I tell you she looked like she was twelve. It's important to note that at the time she was actually sixteen, and I was thirty, so I was still, technically, almost young. And she was, technically, almost an adult. But she looked like a child. The most beautiful, fragile child you ever saw. She wasn't just a child, she was a woman — an incredible, bewitching mixture of both. First of all, and I know this sounds superficial, but there was the dress she wore. I will never forget that dress. It was blue, a medium pale blue somewhere between baby blue, which would have looked too cute, and deep bottom of the sea blue, which would have been boring. It was an indescribable color actually. It had two thin straps, which almost made it seem like it held itself up, and then it was all feathery below the waist, but also swishy and full. It was a Laura Petrie dress — even though I didn't know anything about Laura Petrie at the time. I found out later that in fact it was a designer dress, that she had been modeling part-time and had borrowed it. She didn't wear it like a borrowed dress, she wore it as if she was born to wear it, completely un-self-consciously, which is the way she wore her beauty. She had her hair pulled back, even though it was a natural, pale blond color and obviously beautiful. But there was something about pulling her hair back so modestly that drove me crazy. All it did was accentuate her gigantic eyes.

And then there was the way she moved. It made Andrea seem completely calculated and fake in comparison. There was a hesitance about this new girl, but also a strange assurance. She was caught, hovering, like a fairy, between childhood and adulthood. And I had discovered her at the perfect moment.

Since everyone knows you can't catch a fairy and put her in a jar, I should explain something else. I imagine you might be suspicious of someone thirty years old being attracted to someone who looks twelve. Let me make it clear: she did *look* that young. Physically, she could have been a girl at her first junior-high dance — if she hadn't moved with such bewildering grace. I want to say in my defense that the feeling I had for her, and that I still have for young women in general, is not actually sexual. You may think I protest too much, but I'm not a hypocrite. That's one of the things I hate most and the last thing I would ever be. Ever since I met this girl, ever since I began to be an adult — because for some reason this meeting marks, for me, the moment when I became an adult — I have been attracted to younger women. But that attraction is not physical. And it isn't fetishistic. In fact, calling me a cradle-robbing pervert is as ridiculous as that Bloomingdale's idiot accusing me of being into feet. I wasn't into young girl's bodies, I was into their minds.

Doesn't that make sense?

I want you to think about it for a minute, really think. Here I was trapped at this party by a woman writer who was very much an adult, perhaps ten years older than me, and I was disgusted by what I saw as her predatory, lying manipulations around younger men. All I could see was her hypocrisy, the creeping notion that her intelligence was wrapped up with such silly motives. And I don't blame her. Christ, you shouldn't blame anybody. If I sound like I'm blaming people sometimes — and I know I do — God knows I shouldn't. People can't help the way they are, especially when Christianity and Judaism don't offer real spiritual guidance. People are scarred, they are abused by life and the terrible things it does to them. They do their best to survive, somehow, and if that means taking young writers as lovers and sharing them with one's husband, then so be it. Who am I, and who are you, to judge, or to blame? Most people are doing the best they can. The fact that life offers us all such incredible obstacles doesn't excuse people's maliciousness, but it does make it somewhat understandable.

The thing about young people is that they have rarely had the opportunity to be truly scarred. They are not — aside from exceptional cases of abuse — the walking wounded. They are not, for the most part, lashing out with bitterness, jealousy, and defeat. They are just *being*. They haven't yet learned how *not* to be. Life teaches them that, eventually, and it's one of the most depressing lessons people learn. The reason I fell in love with that girl at that moment on that late summer night was because she was poised between childhood and adulthood. She wasn't a real child. Real children are amazing in their own way, perfect, but you wouldn't want to fall in love with one.

Later I found out that she wasn't as innocent as I believed.

A couple of years earlier she had escaped from a convent, where she had been staying because her parents didn't want her to live with them. Here, I was looking on her as an innocent, and she'd already had one of the primal experiences that an adult has: the most profound of human rejections. Maybe that's why I saw her as so very much on the verge of growing up. But this does tend to be my problem with young people — and I suppose the problem with my stories. I idealize these kids. But if you can't idealize kids, who can you idealize? Adults? At least with young people there's potential. For change, for *something*.

And that's what I saw in Chloe. She was the most *potential* person I had ever met.

How did I get to talk to her? It certainly wasn't difficult.

Our eyes locked, like in *South Pacific*, "somewhere across a crowded room." People used to say that I was strikingly handsome. In moments like that, I wasn't afraid to take advantage of it. I wound my way to her. She was talking to the weary, brilliant husband, which made things easy. I walked right up and greeted him, and naturally he said, "This is Chloe. She's a student at Shipley."

A student at Shipley. Of course, she was young; she would be a student. What else would she be at sixteen? But I'll have to admit that I immediately put glasses on her in my head. I'll tell you, there's something about a girl with glasses, reading a book, which drives me nuts. It's the potential thing. When he said "Shipley" I went crazy imagining her in grassy fields, beside tall old buildings, reading books on summer days. Naturally she would be separate from her friends and from her professors, because she would have to think for herself. That would be the kind of girl she was.

There was nothing to contradict my first impression. She passed every test. Or I guess I should say she passed the first test, which was laughter. She made me laugh, I made her laugh. I can be a really funny guy. I know it might be hard to imagine because I sound so cranky, but I really am funny.

First we talked about how long the apartment was. She talked about how she liked long things. Long books? I said. She said long books were all right as long as they were good books. I had to agree with her. I told her right away about my obsession with books that never ended. It's always been a serious thing with me. When I was young I refused to read a book if it was only one book — there had to be a series. The reason for this was, if it was a good book, I didn't want it to end because that would be too much like someone dying. She understood that right away, how books were like people. You got to know them and like them, she said, and didn't want them to be over. I told her about my two favorite series from when I was a child. First there was the detective pig. He got into different adventures in every book. I can't remember his name now, but he was a great pig — the Sherlock Holmes of the porker set. I told her about how I learned the word "dilemma" from those books, because the pig always got into one. And I told her about my favorite series character, "Timmy," the star of all the *Timmy Books*. Timmy was great. I can't remember much about him either, except that he could jump in the air and click his heels together, three times, before coming down. When I was a kid that amazed me. I tried it myself and could never do it. I almost hurt myself trying. But the fact that Timmy could do it and I couldn't didn't make me believe the story any less, it only increased my admiration for the guy. I read every Timmy book there was, and the only thing that stopped me from committing suicide when I got to the last one — why do writers have to stop writing things? — was realizing I could go back to the beginning and start over, because I'd forgotten the early books.

That made it okay, for a while.

I could tell she was enchanted by my stories. I really can be pretty enchanting sometimes, especially when there's someone like that looking up at me in a perfect blue dress. Then I decided, what the hell, she's really special, I'm going to tell her truth. So I told her I was about to publish a book and I didn't want to talk to any of the creeps at the party. She admitted that they looked pretty creepy to her too. So we started this fabulous game. Chloe was really good at games. Once we played, that was it for me. I was totally gone.

The idea was that every time someone would come near us, we'd start talking about something so horrible, so disgusting that they'd decide it was too awkward to interrupt us. She came up with the idea, which was a great one — that her father was dying of colon cancer. Neither of us had any experience with colon cancer, but we thought it would certainly be one of the most disgusting things and that it would frighten people away. I swear she did the funniest thing when someone would start eyeing us. She'd suddenly say, "And he's dripping from his anus!" It was really shocking. I was actually quite surprised that she could come up with it at her age. And I'd say, "Oh no, not a dripping anus, your father?" Then, when the person turned away, embarrassed — how are you going to break in on a conversation like that? — we'd have to hide our hysteria. It was so much damn fun.

I was impressed. She could be very la-di-da and elegant, but she could also be very silly. Nowadays, I'd compare her to Audrey Hepburn in *Breakfast at Tiffany's*. She looked a lot like her and had the same beguiling mixture of worldliness and grace. Of course it's only with young people that you can make jokes about colon cancer. Most of them haven't experienced colon cancer, and so it really is just a joke. That's one of the things I love about young people. Now, if I bring up colon cancer with another old person, they start talking about remedies, and clucking, and wagging their heads. Her real father — who was already quite old — died only a few years later. I wonder if the horrible illness that killed him was already in the back of her mind.

Anyway, we were having so much fun that I didn't want the party to end. But she was just sixteen, so it didn't seem right to keep her up too late. Yes, I was aware that she was too young for me to actually start anything — I'm not that kind of creep — but I figured that if I gave her my address, we could keep in touch. The time I spent with her was like experiencing a great book. When you realize a book is great, you don't want to read too fast. Great books are usually too short — I have a fondness for shorter books, short stories really, which is a problem — you know that someday the end is going to come, and it's going to be too soon. So you put that book down, or even put it away, for a day or two. When it's time to pick it up again, you only read a little bit and savor it. Then you can walk around for the whole day, knowing that the book is waiting for you, and thinking of how good it will be. That's what happened to me after meeting Chloe.

Whenever I fall in love, I feel like Gene Kelly in *Singing in the Rain*. People love the famous scene in that movie so much because it perfectly captures the feeling of just leaving someone you love. You haven't really made out with them or anything, maybe you've only kissed them, but you've got a vision of them, the feeling of them, maybe even the smell of them inside you. And you feel so happy, you want to run around and stomp your feet in puddles with joy.

I thought if I gave her my address, we might start a correspondence. It would be an appropriate way for us to relate until she grew up a little — for decency's sake. But I have to admit I was looking forward to the prospect of exchanging letters. It's the most wonderful kind of relationship to have — an epistolary one. Contrary to what most people think, you can get inside someone quite easily when you communicate in letters. I suppose that, technically speaking, it's possible to lie in letters, but it seems to me that the truth always comes through, even if it's just between the lines.

So we started writing to each other. Her first letters were so damn charming. She called me The Great Writer because I had just finished a book. I should have been irritated because she hadn't read anything I'd written, but coming from a sixteen year old it was charming. She wrote a great deal about her parents. They were amazing people. They'd come to the United States as refugees during the war, but they were cultured, which certainly explained why she was such a special girl. Her father was a relatively famous art critic, and expert on Fra Angelico. I'm not quite sure what that is. I'm not into the whole fine art thing, but it would certainly explain why she was so mature for her age. Naturally, there was also resentment towards her parents, because they had lived all those war years in New York and left her in foster homes. That was the weirdest thing. First of all, why would they want to be separated from such a beautiful, intelligent daughter? And secondly, even if they hated her or hated kids, how could such a thing be legal? But it was, and to add insult to injury, when the war was over and she came back to live with them in New York, they put her in a convent. I tried to make her understand, it was my first spiritual lesson for her, that you can't blame people for being horrible. And that you can't spend your whole life being tortured and bitter. I mean, my upbringing was classic. I had the kind of mother who loves you too much, who doesn't have a life outside of you. She actually called me "Sonny." Like in the old Al Jolson movies. My sister says that the fact that she doted on me so much did me irreparable harm. I know I'm completely nuts in some ways, so maybe it has something to do with her. In her eyes I could do no wrong. If I told her I'd killed a guy in cold blood, she'd probably assume I had good reason and make me dinner.

Anyway, the letters went great, for almost a whole year. We used to meet now and then and have coffee, and every time I saw her I'd go crazy over how beautiful she was. But two things began to get in the way of what I saw as a perfect relationship. One was my desire, and the other was that she was planning on going to university.

We should deal with the university thing first, because it's complicated.

The one thing I hate more than jazz is universities. I'm sure you could say it has something to do with getting kicked out of prep school, which wasn't a pleasant experience. But it's much more than that. It's the whole idea of them. I know I said earlier that when I first fell in love with Chloe I imagined her reading a book at some university. But remember, I said . . . *out on the lawn, away from everyone else.* I'm a great believer in home schooling actually, and I would have done it with my own kids if, well, Chloe had let me. But that's another story. Also, if you haven't realized already, I contradict myself now and then. On the one hand, I'll say that I hate something and then I'll turn around and say something nice about it. It's the same thing with people, and I think it can be explained by my overly romantic nature. For instance, I actually do, in one way, like the *idea* of jazz. I like the idea of a form of music that is inspiring, that touches people in unexpected ways. But that's not what jazz is. I also like the idea of what most people *might* be, I like their *potential.* But I don't like what happens to most of them in real life. I like what I imagine things to be, but I don't usually like what they are.

Also, it's my plan — and yes I do have one — to write this non-stop, without revision. Okay, sure, I might revise for style. Every comma has to be in place. (I'm no Kerouac.) But not for content. I'm not going back over this for instance, and saying, "But earlier I said . . ." so I can't say *whatever* now. Like some stupid editor would do. That's one of the worst problems with editors actually. They don't understand that real people contradict themselves and change their minds. They want characters to be consistent. Excuse me, people aren't.

So, I hate universities with a passion. I like the idea of learning, but I don't like institutions — I don't like institutionalized anything. Eastern religions aren't based on institutions; they are based on people having private experiences. And that's what learning is, or should be: a private experience. The idea of someone standing up in front of you and being an expert is a lie. I guess some people know more facts. But facts don't mean anything when divorced from experience. And most of these damn teachers don't even clean their ears. Have you ever noticed how most teachers are physically disgusting? I know we're supposed to forgive them because their heads are in the clouds and they're so damn brilliant, but what does it take to trim your nose hair? If you can't do that, buddy, then you shouldn't be teaching anybody anything.

Learning is pretty simple. You don't need to go to university; all you need to do is read. And then go back to life, and then read again. Compare the experience that you get from books with the experience you get from life. Sometimes the two match up; sometimes they don't. But it's by comparing the two that you learn. If you take away one — either the books or the real life — then you're only getting half an education. All universities give you is the learning from books, which is useless without the real-life experience.

The uselessness of universities is exemplified by the Section Man. What's a Section Man? A sporty-looking teacher, somebody who's trying to get ahead by learning everything they can about a tiny, irrelevant subject nobody cares about.

They say they're contributing to our knowledge about under-researched subjects, but that's a load of bilge. I am, for example, absolutely suspicious of the whole idea of a science of literature, the whole idea of studying English. It was considered too effete, too silly and inconsequential, to be a fit subject for study in the nineteenth century. Then a wrong-headed guy by the name of F.R. Leavis came up with something called the New Criticism, which was essentially the idea that literature could be studied like a science.

I've got news for you F.R., you can't do it. You might as well learn to live with the fact that real literature can't be analyzed or explained. That's why I hate James Joyce and T.S. Eliot. They were a product of this, the same way modern jazz is a result of music critics and historians who are too smart for their own damn good. What happens is some artists read the criticism — because deep down they're nothing but Section Men themselves — and then they try to produce art that fits into the critic's idea of profound work. In the case of Joyce and Eliot, this included footnoting their own work through classical references and allusions. Section Men will be analyzing *Ulysses* for the next century.

I used to meet Section Men at *New Yorker* parties. The main thing I noticed is that I made them uncomfortable. They'd come up to me, just to chat, you know, and then they'd figure out I was a writer, or maybe they'd heard of me, and then they would try to act casual — these guys were always casual, never excited or passionate — and ask me, as an offhand question, "So, listen, you have to tell me, what ultimately are you trying to get at with your writing?" You think I answered them? I knew they'd run back to their undergraduate students or their Ph.D. advisors and say, "I was talking to a writer I met at a party. Now he *claimed* to be a passionate person. He *claimed* that he loved writing. In his case, writing definitely seemed to be a repository for the self. Here, I think we see the failure of the psychoanalytic approach to literature. The man was obviously in need of a good shrink."

Yeah, well, I think you're in need of a good beheading. There I was, standing in front of these guys, feeling like my pants were pulled down around my ankles, because I was an artist, and I was expressing myself, revealing everything the way artists do, and there they were chuckling away irrepressibly, and waving their hands, saying, "Sorry . . . sorry, I just found what you said so funny. . . . Go on. . . . You think writing is a vocation? You're passionate about it? That's fascinating, go on, go on. . . ." As you can see, I've had experience with these guys, and the truth is they are terrified of real emotion, real ideas, real passion — scared to death. They use their crappy theories and jargon to keep that fear at bay.

As soon as Chloe mentioned Radcliffe, I got myself into a state. All I could think about was the busload of Section Men who'd be lining up to screw her. Smart as she was, I knew she'd be susceptible. Back in the forties, the problem with those Section Men was that someone made the mistake of informing them that the only reason university professors weren't getting laid was because they didn't keep themselves clean. So suddenly these academic types started to spruce themselves up and take baths. The only difference was this: when teaching English wasn't all that respectable, it only attracted the ordinary nerds who didn't use deodorant and forgot to wash their feet. But once those Section jobs became especially high-paying gigs, the English professor types went all natty, and mustachioed, and lean, and — with their long fingers and detached chuckles — the young girls went for that. I wish I could explain it; I suppose it's not any more horrible than the feelings I had back then about girls in pretty skirts.

———

Yeah. Desire. As I was getting to know Chloe, I was also exploring Eastern religion in a significant way. In fact, the idea of becoming a monk occurred to me. I know it might sound crazy, but I still find a monk's life appealing. First of all, you don't have to see anyone except other monks. And since you can go someplace and take a vow of silence, you don't even have to talk to them. I could imagine myself picking peas all day long, or feeding hogs, or meditating. To me it would be almost perfect. I'd have to write, definitely. But I could put it away in a drawer and not let anyone read it, except maybe God.

I could even get into the robes and prayers. I'm sure there must be a monk's code or something, a way they deal with each other. Even without a code of silence, I could be the silent monk. That might even be my name. Brother Dumb. That's what they'd call me. I'd be Brother Dumb, and people would respect my need to be left alone — the way they respect a deaf person.

The thing I really like about the idea of being a monk is that I don't mind being around people now and then, in controlled situations. I just like to be able to keep my distance.

That's why the post office in town is such a perfect place. I *have* to go there once a day, but I know I'm only going to meet one or two people, and most of them are true New Englanders, so they only look at me grumpily, and say things like, "Did you get that stone wall repaired?"

I know they don't want to talk either, but they have to, which is something I identify with. And then they quote Robert Frost, "You know, 'good fences make good neighbors.'" And then they say, "A-yep" — a New England expression of agreement — and trundle on their solitary way.

Anyway, this was the life I was contemplating. Being a monk, there would be no temptation. No indescribably blue dresses swirling around sixteen-year-old girls' knees. None. You wouldn't be liable to find that kind of thing at a monastery. But I don't want you to think I'm puritanical. Judaism and Christianity are generally puritanical and I hate that. There's nothing wrong with sex, it's not dirty. Sex is great, as I'm sure any guy will tell you. The problem is that desire, like greed and vanity, is a worldly concern. And all worldly concerns ultimately lead to pain. If you've ever experienced any of these things, you'll know how closely connected they are. For me, greed's not a big issue. This is probably because I never wanted for anything as a child. My father managed a huge meat-packing concern, and we were never short on money. My parents helped me out until I was almost thirty. I led a relatively privileged life, and because of that I never became obsessed with money. By the time I was ready to move out of the house, I was lucky enough to be earning a living from my stories. All I ever needed was enough to get by on, and as I've gotten older I haven't found it difficult to whittle down my personal possessions to the bare essentials.

Vanity, however, is something I struggle with — as you can probably tell. I tend to get angry when people don't like my work. But there are times, like right now, when I'm relatively calm, and I think, sensibly, that you can't please all of the people all of the time. Jesus, sometimes I believe my mother loved me too much. It's hard for me to take criticism. I have to remember that I'm not in any way perfect and never will be. The hardest thing of all would be for me to say that maybe I'm a lousy writer.

That's a difficult thing for me to even put on a page. But if you're going to become egoless, you have to. And when it comes right down to it, it's the experience of writing that keeps you going, not whether or not somebody likes it. I don't know if I would still be alive if I didn't have this book to write, for instance. Maybe I am a lousy writer. Who cares?

But when it comes to sexual desire? That's more difficult. Because, like gluttony, desire is physical. I've never had a problem with gluttony, in fact for the past few years I've been into macrobiotics. I don't need much anyway, because I have a lean body type. Food has never been an issue. I enjoy semi-starving myself and eating pure. There's nothing greater, actually, than a feeling of emptiness. It means you're healthy.

I wish I could say the same about sexual desire. The problem is you don't want to be hungry with desire. If you go without, you don't get used to it the way you do when you starve yourself of food. You just want more. And my problem too, is that I need a young woman around because I get lonely. I certainly wouldn't want a young man around, my son being the obvious exception. Even though my attraction to young women is mainly spiritual and platonic, I'm a man, and sooner or later those desires come up. And, well, what are you going to do?

When I first met Chloe, everything worked out great. I realized I probably shouldn't become physically involved with her because of her age. But by the time she finally started going to Radcliffe — as much as I railed against Section Men, there was nothing I could do to stop her — she was eighteen and old enough for us to have sex.

I found myself going mad, thinking about the possibility.

Radcliffe is in Cambridge, so I had to take the train to see her. The hotel I decided to stay at was called the Commodore. I picked it for the same reason I pick all hotel rooms, for their suicidal possibilities. As I've said, a hotel isn't home and it shouldn't try to be: it should be, simply, as lean and mean as possible. The Commodore was like that, with its military feel, swords and hats on display, and the odd ship in a bottle. Funny, that in such a military place, I would experience such intense pangs of sexual desire. I won't go into the crass details, but it became torturous. I even took to buying magazines. I had promised myself that I wasn't going to have sex with Chloe, because that would start an endless cycle of want, and need, and debasement of my feelings for her. Which *were* completely pure, in their essence, I swear. But, Jesus, after we'd go out for a coffee and a walk, I'd find myself picking up a girlie magazine of all things. And then it wasn't long before I was back at the Commodore, all alone, with the swords and the military regalia, doing what was necessary. I struggled with those sexual feelings. For a while, I would buy the magazine after meeting Chloe, then go up to my room. . . . Then I'd throw it in the garbage. I was careful to dump it far from the hotel in case someone found it. That's how nuts I was. I mean, I bought a girlie magazine and did what everyone does. Big deal. But the idea was not to have the magazine around as a continual temptation. I wanted to get it out of my hands, so to speak.

After the Commodore visits became a kind of ritual, I decided to turn my life into an Edward Hopper painting. It was a strange thing to do, but I couldn't resist. Have you ever done anything like that? Taken characters from literature or art, and tried to make yourself into them?

My favorite painting had always been Hopper's *Nighthawks*. So I decided to turn myself into the guy in the painting who is sitting at the end of the counter with his back to you. The one all alone, across from the redhead. That painting expressed my whole dilemma. (See, I do know how to use the word "dilemma" now.) There was that lonely guy, drinking his coffee. But you just know he wants to jump the bones of the redhead sitting beside the other guy. I assumed the lonely guy was spiritual, like me. That he was saving himself for something. His next life, maybe. The other guy — the one sitting beside the redhead — represented my enforced celibacy, since in the painting he is the obstacle to the other two getting together. It was all very symbolic. Anyway, I found a café like the one in Hopper's painting in Boston. After I'd had dinner with Chloe, I'd go get my girlie mag and do my thing, and then I'd brazenly leave the magazine in the hotel room — which was a big deal for me, knowing it would be there, waiting for me, when I got back. Then I'd go to the all-night diner that looked like the one in *Nighthawks*, and I'd sit there sipping my coffee like the guy in the painting, knowing I was going home to "read."

For a while, I told myself I was doing everything in my power to resist having sex with Chloe. If that meant becoming a character from a painting, so be it. It was, after all, a small price to pay. Around this time I also decided to tell her that I didn't think it was a good idea for us to have sex. On one hand, I didn't want her to think that I didn't love her, or that I was a flit. On the other, I figured she would be able to join me in this resolve. We had already talked a lot about spirituality and the need to get rid of ego, greed, and gluttony. So I explained that getting rid of sexual desire was necessary too. She didn't understand at first, and I could tell she was disappointed. I said for a while, until I got used to it, we could still kiss, but it wouldn't be a good idea for us to do anything else. She reluctantly agreed.

But soon I realized I was turning into a kind of sex-obsessed fiend. Was it possible that prohibiting myself from having sex with Chloe had made me more concerned with sex than I would have been if I was actually doing it with her? I finally argued myself into the idea that I could have sex with her once in a while — let's say once a month or something — just to get it out of my system. I decided to tell her that I was going nuts, and that it *would* be a good idea for us to have sex now and then. She looked at me as if to say, "What are you making such a fuss about?" And she was right. That's what killed me. You know, with some people, it's a lot easier to be pure. It's like they're born without ego and without desire, the way I was born without greed or gluttony. Why should some people be free of all the worst of the worldly passions? I guess they're simply reincarnations of a higher level of consciousness and you have to accept it.

Whatever I decided would be okay with Chloe — she was so enamored. This was one of the reasons I loved her: she was so malleable and agreeable and non-pressuring. I really need to be in that kind of an environment. I won't go into the details, because it's not appropriate, but we finally did get down to it one night. The problem was, it was so good that I went even more nuts. I started going to Cambridge every week, just so we could do it. Actually, I knew that would happen. Soon, however, I started resenting Chloe, because to me, as beautiful and bright as she was, she suddenly represented sex. I knew that was going to happen, as well. How do people deal with that part of intimacy? I've never understood. Here's this person you idealize, who you're totally in love with, and then you're supposed to go to them to get your darkest deepest needs fulfilled? It's not that those needs are so awful, it's just, well, if you need them for that kind of thing you can't help but associate them with it.

On top of all this, two years after I first met her, Chloe got offered a summer job working as a model. When she got the offer, I was really surprised. She didn't tell me that she had any modeling connections. It was then that she mentioned how she got the dress she wore to the party. I found the whole modeling thing a little suspect. First of all, I wasn't really pleased that the world at large would be looking at magazine pictures of the woman I loved. I mean, look at me and the girlie mags. How could I be sure that guys wouldn't be doing that to pictures of her? And secondly, modeling itself was something that appealed to vanity and ego. She was a beautiful girl. But she had me to tell her she was beautiful, and that was out of love. Wasn't all this stuff with store-bought dresses and magazine pictures just more worldly crap? I could tell she didn't agree, but she still promised she wouldn't model. Somehow, though, she had all the money she needed that summer. . . . I didn't see her every day, only on weekends, so I was suspicious. Chloe had always had a will of her own, which is, I guess, part of what attracted me.

All this made me associate her with the worldliness I was trying to escape. Yes, my novel appeared, and so did the movie. The film was a flop — which makes sense, because it was very bad. The novel was a huge hit — which makes sense, because it was very good. It was hard for me not to get excited about the success of my book. You try getting a rave review in *Time* when you're barely thirty.

I wound up thinking about getting a house somewhere off in the country, away from everything. I drove around Massachusetts on the way up to see Chloe, and found this little town in New Hampshire that wasn't a town at all.

I should probably tell you what made me fall in love with the house. It was in the middle of nowhere. There was no town to speak of, just a general store with a post office and the firehouse. You gotta have a firehouse. I liked my remote little place so much because it represented, perfectly, the idea of a humble, spiritual man and his imagination.

The house itself was almost nothing. A shack. Ram-shackle. No bathroom, and only a sink for a kitchen. There was a tiny little room on the main floor that was supposed to be a bedroom, and then a gigantic living room that looked like an old barn, with a ceiling two storeys high and a huge fireplace. Everything was falling apart. There was a tiny loft space above, up a high, narrow ladder, which could also be used for sleeping. But when you opened the window . . .

First you would see a vast, grassy meadow that fell steeply to the Connecticut River. Beyond the river, the meadow went for acres and acres, until it reached the mountain that domi-. nated the skyline. To the right, little farmhouses dotted the hills, which, eventually, rolled into the Adirondacks.

I began to think of that house as a man — someone pure, who had rid himself of all earthly desire, who didn't care about how he appeared. From the inside, when the window was open — his imagination . . . it was breathtaking. This is why I had to buy it. I certainly had enough money rolling in. I couldn't wait to ask Chloe to move in with me. I had it all figured out: my real problem was that I was compressing too much into my time with Chloe, seeing her only once a week. If we lived together, maybe desire wouldn't be such a big deal. And because I associated the house with purity, with spiritu- ality, I figured that when Chloe joined me, our relationship would become more spiritual too.

I didn't count on her turning me down.

Her refusal had mainly to do with the fact that she didn't want to drop out of Radcliffe. It didn't make any sense to me. At the time she was mostly reading books I had suggested — spiritual books — and so it wasn't like she was dedicated to her studies or even enjoying them. When she said she wanted to wait until she graduated, I completely lost my mind. Again.

I got on my high horse. That's something I'm prone to — as you may have figured out. The danger, if you've managed to push material things away, is that you might take too much pride in *not* being worldly and then lord it over others. I think I'm more conscious of that trap now. I really do try to keep my self-righteousness under control. But back then it was my first experience with the idea of cleansing my life of everything impure.

I didn't get mad, I just disappeared. It wasn't that difficult. I bought the house in New Hampshire, and moved everything out of my black apartment in Greenwich Village. There wasn't much to move anyway. Finally, I was able to live my life's dream: to be completely alone. It was heaven, at first. There was a lot of work, of course, and I would divide my day between three things I loved: renovating, clearing the land, and writing. It was Spartan. I made an effort to not be too proud — to merely enjoy the work itself as work. Every morning I would get up and write for five hours, then take a little break to sit outside looking at the Connecticut River. Later, I'd eat farm vegetables from the local store. In the afternoon, I would start on other chores, working in the garden or on the house.

Everything was great. I was self-sufficient, and didn't seem to need Chloe, or miss her. But then, suddenly, I did. Worldly lust? Or was it love? I wasn't sure.

My first clue? What I was writing turned out to be about her. The story of a spiritual girl and her creepy Section Man boyfriend. I can't tell you how much fun I had writing the Section Man. Even though I wasn't willing to admit it to myself, I was going to sleep every night thinking about Chloe ending up with some smooth-talking creep who specialized in nineteenth-century dramatic narratives.

Okay, yeah, I know. I haven't sufficiently described Chloe's brilliance, or what made me love her.

———

Chloe wasn't the smartest woman I'd ever loved — I don't mean she was stupid, she wasn't — but she was the funniest. By "funniest" I mean she could see right into the heart of things, to where the humor was. You see, everything is funny, in its own way. Actually, that's also what God is. If you ever wondered how you'll recognize God, well, you'll only make the discovery if you have a sense of humor. Before Chloe moved into the girls' dormitory at Radcliffe, for instance, she stayed in a flat in an old house in downtown Cambridge. It wasn't a great part of town. Let's just say there was quite a mixture of people living there, including those who were truly down and out. One day, Chloe was planting a flower box to cheer the place up — she was always doing things like that — when the woman next door was dragged away in handcuffs. Her roommate, or boyfriend, or whatever, had accused her of being a thief. The way Chloe told the story was hilarious. Apparently the woman was in her best dress — which made Chloe think she had gotten all dolled up to get arrested. This woman smoked all the time and had a very deep voice. Chloe described it as "a gravel truck unloading," which was exactly right. When the gal was arrested, Chloe told me she said, "I'm calling my mother! I'm going to call my mother!" Anyway, Mom must have been an even worse monster, because the policeman said, "Not that, baby. Please, not that." I know, at first this might not seem funny — only cruel. But it's important to recognize that Chloe had an eye for the ridiculous in herself as well. Sometimes she called herself a pampered poodle, or a sad little Shetland pony. "Poor little rich girl," she would say with some irony. And it was ironic, because she had nothing to complain about financially — it was just that her parents had treated her like dirt. She knew the only thing she had to worry about was emotional deprivation — something only the rich could afford. Regardless of whether Chloe laughed at the gravel-voiced woman, or at herself, she understood basic humanity. That's what made it godly.

When I was first in New Hampshire, before I got completely into the healthy eating, I used to drive to another small town that actually had a diner, to have lunch sometimes, before my afternoon chores. There was a wispy sort of waitress there who served all the old guys — they were mainly old guys — and she always tried to make conversation. This was difficult, because in New England conversation doesn't come easy. One day, I guess one of the regulars had died, and she was going on about how incredibly cranky he was. She said a great thing, "I imagine God would be frightened to meet him." And then she took it further, "I bet the devil would be frightened too."

When one of the old men chimed in about what a scary character the dead guy was, she said, "Let me tell you, you wouldn't want to be the one to tell him there was no rice pudding." Even though I was supposed to be committed to solitude, I wanted to run and tell Chloe that one, you know?

Thinking about the Section Man, who probably didn't have insane issues with celibacy — Section Men aren't pure,

they only want to get ahead — meant imagining him screw-
ing Chloe regularly. It made me want to pound my head into
a wall. And when Chloe told him one of her funny stories,
I'm sure the guy would say, "Oh, that's very droll," and then
turn away to finish his Waldorf salad, not realizing he'd
missed a little glimpse of God. (To a Section Man, God is a
tenure-track appointment.) Anyway, the story I was writing
was all about Chloe, which meant Chloe had become my new
best friend. And since I had been writing about her every day
for months on end, it was like being with her in a fantasy —
and it wasn't healthy.

Then there was the incident with the girls. When I ate lunch
at the restaurant, a few young girls would hang out at the
counter. It was all teenage stuff. I didn't pay much attention,
until the day one of them came up to me.

"Excuse me sir, may I ask you a question?"

"Sure."

"You don't look like the kind of guy who usually comes
in here." There were giggles from the soda counter.

"No?"

"No."

"What do you mean?"

"I mean, like the usual old guys." Giggles again.

"I'm not that old."

"We wondered if you lived around here."

"Yes, I do."

"What do you do?"

"I'm a writer."

I felt I could be honest because they were nice kids. What was not to like? They seemed sweet, innocent, and without ulterior motives. I'd say "hi" to them, just to be nice, and then one day one of the girls — she wore glasses but wasn't too homely — came over with a pad and pencil. She told me she had to write an article for the school newspaper about local personalities, and she wondered if she could interview me. I said sure. By this time I'd decided not to give real interviews — I was doing everything I could do to get away from the fame thing. I wouldn't even allow an author photo on the paperback edition of my novel. But I thought, gee whiz, this is a little school newspaper in New Hampshire, what's the big deal?

Her questions were the usual ones. Why do you write, and where do you get your ideas, and what inspires you? Actually, those are the hardest questions to answer. But because she was earnest, I tried to be as truthful as possible, and probably revealed a little too much of myself in the process. After that, whenever the girls were in the diner the one with the glasses would come over to talk. She asked me to give her some advice about writing. What with the glasses, and her being a budding writer and everything, you guessed it, I was attracted to her. I knew it was crazy, the girl was barely fifteen — not even as old as Chloe was when we met. But in the back of my mind I also knew that the reason I was becoming a bit obsessed with her was because I had cut Chloe out of my life. I didn't have time to become conflicted about it, however, because our friendship was cut short.

The article she wrote for the school newspaper wound up in *Time*.

God, I was furious. And disappointed. Then I realized, you know, there's no point in getting mad at her. What does she know? She was obviously manipulated by some guy, some old creep, probably her father, who convinced her to sell the story for extra cash. But it seriously shook my confidence in my ability to make new friends, especially with young people. I guess I took it as a sign, in a way, that I had deprived myself by pushing Chloe out of my life. But this happened early on in The Year Without Chloe, and I tried to put it all in the back of my mind.

I made one last concerted effort to live utterly alone. I worked on my story and my house, and I committed myself to healthy eating. After the incident with the teenagers at the restaurant, this was easy; that little hick-town diner came to represent the evil that was out there. Eating healthily is the key to happiness, a better life, and calmness of spirit and everything. If you think the whole idea of me getting so excited about dietary concerns funny, you should stop and think about what *you* eat.

Consider milk. You are aware that human beings were not meant to drink a cow's milk, right? Cows' milk is for baby cows, like human breast milk is for human babies. How healthy do you think it would be for an elephant or a tiger to drink a human mother's breast milk? Besides, the way they treat cows these days, the way they torture them, all sorts of vile stuff gets in there. You should see these poor cows, they get so bloated. All that milk is painful, sad, and disgusting.

Anyway, what you end up with, in your milk, is blood and pus. That's what you're drinking, all mixed in with your yummy white stuff.

Humans were meant to live on nuts and berries, that's what we can digest. We get all the nutrients we need from them, and they're not carcinogenic. If you wonder about why there are so many different cancers these days, you might want to start reading the back of a pack of crackers. Tri-sorbitate this and polyunsaturated that. It's all fats and calories — and unhealthy crap that will kill you.

I'm telling you this so you'll know. There's no excuse, now, for mistreating yourself. I'm living proof, because I'm an old man and I feel fine most of the time. Sure, you can talk about good genes, but there's more to it than that. The care you take makes a huge difference. If you get sick and die, you only have yourself to blame. I know that sounds harsh, but you have to take care of yourself and treat the entire medical profession with skepticism. Doctors are far from perfect. I had to go into a doctor's office when my daughter was having emotional problems. I couldn't get over the pharmaceutical ads, ads scattered here and there on the counter, for anti-depressive drugs. Do you realize that even sugar is a drug, an unnatural substance? That you could smooth out that emotional rollercoaster in a second by cutting down on that nasty upper? Doctors shouldn't be prescribing drugs for mood swings; they should start by changing dietary habits. The medical profession overprescribes — antibiotics may work for mass epidemics, but they should not be taken on a regular basis. I'm convinced that the overprescription of antibiotics has caused both a rash of new diseases and the return of old ones. You should let your body's immune system take care of itself.

Okay, lecture over.

———

After nearly a year of making myself healthy and writing about Chloe, I finally finished the story. I wasn't about to go through what I went through with my novel. I was never going to say goodbye to a character again, it was simply too painful. With the incident with the diner kid in the back of my mind, I figured the only thing I could do was go back, tail between my legs, to Chloe. Maybe I wasn't the type of guy who could live in complete seclusion — maybe I had to have a beautiful girl beside me, blue dress or not.

During my year alone I had managed to find spiritual support for my decision. The Ramakrishna was a true ascetic, and there was no room in his cosmology for those who were not willing to give up the world. As much as I wanted to give it up, I was sure having a lot of trouble. In my reading, I happened to stumble on Paramahansa Yogananda's *Autobiography of a Yogi*, which had some interesting stories about a guy named Lahiri Mahasaya. He was a true yogi, yet he also represented those who are pure of heart but find themselves encumbered by worldly things, even though they try, valiantly, to detach themselves. This discovery was like hitting the jackpot. God understood that there were guys like me, guys whose true goal was to be Brother Dumb, but who couldn't quite make it. It was possible to have a wife and family and still be spiritual.

Now, you might think that this was a matter of putting the cart before the horse, of finding justification for my weaknesses. I guess it was. But what can you do? I never claimed to be anything but an imperfect human — which is a redundancy, actually — but I still wanted to achieve enlightenment. Anyway, I figured, if not in this life, then in another. Nobody said living wouldn't be a struggle.

When I figured this out I called Chloe. As you can imagine, she was surprised to hear from me. It turned out she'd had a difficult year. After I disappeared, she wound up in hospital, which made me feel awful. Still, if my rejection of the world hurt her that much, she must have really loved me.

The extremely weird thing was that while I was away Chloe had gotten married. By the time I called, however, the marriage had been annulled. Thank Christ! At first, it was a bit much for me. The thing about annulments, as I understand them, is they're different from a divorce; the couple hasn't actually consummated anything. That was my understanding, anyway. It was difficult for me to come to terms with it, but when Chloe explained that she thought I had rejected her forever, and that she was at her wit's end, literally, when this pushy idiot started visiting her in the hospital — I felt a lot better.

Visiting was more than I had done. Thank God he turned out to be a business student, not a Section Man. She also told me that he was a complete goof, and she felt sorry for him — which, even though it's not a good reason to marry, does have a spiritual ring to it. I forgave her because I loved her, and because she said something important. When I was haranguing her, she said, "Life goes on." And that touched me deeply.

It really made me think about death, because when you're a true hermit, it's as if you've died.

Do you ever think about what will happen when you die? What about all the people who love you? The answer, of course, is: life goes on. Years later I always find myself thinking of people who've died. There I am, living life without them, when I wonder what it would be like for them to be around, and what it must be like for them to miss everything that happens, all these great occurrences and revelations. But the point is, we all die, and everything continues. It seems relentless and cruel, but it's actually the point. When I looked at myself as having died for a year, I didn't mind Chloe getting married quite so much, and I felt I could forgive her.

She had just started her final term at Radcliffe, and even though it wasn't easy for her to leave school, I explained to her all about renunciation — how the hardest things to give up are the best, for the soul. It's like Eastern religion is one big Lent. They don't wait for a few weeks in April; they do it all their lives. It was winter, and very cold, but we managed to find a justice of the peace and get married. Settling down in our little hermitage didn't prove to be as easy as I had hoped, because it was pretty clear from the start that Chloe, unfortunately, found renunciation a lot more difficult than I did. I could tell that she missed college life, and parties, and probably modeling. I'm sure she had been lying to me and doing it on the side. Most of her dissatisfactions were around living the cloistered life. I tried to explain to her that we were like monks, and for a while she liked the idea, but she couldn't really commit herself to it. The fact was that she needed people, and I didn't.

I'm afraid I don't have much sympathy for her point of view. Once she said, "I think you're more introverted than I am. I'm an extrovert." I suppose I should think of that as a difference, like being born with webbed toes or something. But try as I might to see extroverts and introverts as separate but equal, I can't. Sure, I suppose it's possible that liking people or not liking people is something you're born with, and there's nothing anyone can do about it. And I certainly admit that it was easy enough for someone like me to give up people, because I hate everyone, generally, even though I try my best not to. But that's the thing, if I see people in small doses, I *can* love them. One by one is easier. In groups, I want to get a gun and start shooting. But it's not just a matter of genetics, is it? Isn't the need for people a worldly need? Something else you have to give up if you want to be pure? And as much as you might say that people go to parties to laugh and have fun, it really is about something else. It's about getting approval. Psychiatrists have proved it. I've read things that say that extroverts only feel real when they are with others. That's sick. The whole point is, you have to learn how to be real when you're by yourself. You know, the "if a tree falls in the woods does anybody hear it?" sort of thing. You exist, even if no one else perceives you. You exist because you are God's work of art. In that way, you are not real at all, because you are a figment of somebody's imagination. But since that somebody is God, it means you *are* real.

I tried to explain all this to Chloe. Because she's not stupid, she got it. But understanding something and living something are very different. I knew that we were in trouble after the Faces incident.

The Faces were wonderful. I met Judge Face at a party in New York, but like me, he and his wife had moved to the country. They were the only people I could bear to entertain. Chloe seemed to like them, but I think it was only out of desperation. At one point, I asked her what she really thought, and she made a very bad, very Chloe pun.

"Well, they are faces," she said, "it's nice to see a couple of different ones once in a while."

I guess she never truly understood why the Faces were so important to me.

One night we had the Faces over for dinner. Sure, they were a lot older than Chloe, being in their seventies. But I don't understand why age is an issue. Goodness, sweetness and wit transcend age, don't they? So Mrs. Face wasn't what you'd call an exciting character, so what? Judge Face was the one with all the personality. But you could see she really appreciated her husband, and got all his jokes. I can't really say enough about the Judge. First of all, he was one of the most distinguished jurists in America. And I hope you know me well enough by now to know that I don't mean famous, or well-respected. A lot of people hated him, actually, and he had been passed over for a place on the Supreme Court because of his controversial views. When I say he was distinguished, I mean he was distinguished to me, and I'm sure he was distinguished in the eyes of God. Anyway, Judge Face's controversial theory about the law was that, ultimately, there was no right and wrong. There was only a discussion of a certain situation, and the judgment of peers — either juries or men like himself. In other words, everything was relative. I know this might sound wacky, but it really was about trusting in the goodness of people, or the justness of their arguments and discussions. Whenever we argued, for instance, he'd say, "That's good, we're arguing, that means we're getting closer to the truth." But if we agreed, he'd say, "This is horrible, we've come to a consensus, before you know it, we'll be writing law." He wasn't saying that there shouldn't be laws, only that as soon as things became law, they should be argued against and constantly put to the test. In a world ruled by Judge Face, laws would be challenged and healthy skepticism would triumph over fascist certainty. I guess I identified with him because his ideas were unpopular with his peers, but also because he was always right — something Judge Face himself would have denied, of course.

The other thing that distinguished the Judge was his love of literature. There aren't many people who really *love* literature, get their sustenance from it, their life's blood. There are people who read because they have to, or because it furthers their careers, or because they think it makes them appear intelligent. My sister, for instance, is crazy for murder mysteries. It's real love, there's no pretension in it. I think she's read every mystery that's ever been written, especially the ones by Jim Thompson, but I'm not too sure she's read all my books. And I haven't written all that much. I forgive her, because her love of books actually keeps her alive. She also adores kid's books. She goes back and reads the books she loved as a child over and over. To a trained psychologist, this might indicate that she's caught in a demented time warp. I really don't care.

The thing that gets me is that she has to go back to Nancy Drew or *A Wrinkle in Time* now and then, just to experience the joy she felt before. She reads to nourish her soul. In the best way, she reminds me of those sad ladies on the subway you see reading romance novels. Are they really sad? You know, the wrinkly, sweaty, disgusting-looking women who have given up on being attractive. God knows what their husbands look like. Most of them probably don't have husbands, or else their guy is a drunk or in jail. But they read their romance novels, with the lurid covers, where the girls are always being swept off to a castle by a muscled guy on a silver steed. Pornography? Maybe. Not real life — living instead a life borrowed from literature? Sure. But sometimes I'm not convinced real life is the real thing at all.

Judge Face had the same kind of dedication to books that my sister has to mysteries and the old ladies on the subway have for romances. But he had better taste. He was a big fan of Tolstoy, Kafka, and Chekhov — just like me. On the night in question, the one I'm telling you about, we were reading stuff aloud, like we'd always do. The chosen work was *The Seagull*. Judge Face was sitting on the couch, reading one of those speeches by Trigorin or whatever the guy's name was, and his wife was beside him, lapping up every bit of it. Chloe and I were in chairs facing them — only Chloe had her legs slung over the side of hers, which to me, was a tad irreverent. I don't mean to say that we all had to act like we were in church or something, or that appreciating literature is like organized religion. I don't mean that. But she obviously had some sort of bee in her bonnet, and when Chloe had a bee, something was likely to explode. So Judge Face was reading this great speech, and he read it very well. It was one of those speeches you only find in Chekhov, but they're all over his work. They say that great artists are always writing the same thing, only in different ways. That's why it doesn't bug me when I write a book and they say, *Oh, he's on about the same old thing. . . .* Of course I am. What else am I going to be on about? Anyway, it was one of those speeches where the guy is talking about the new world there was going to be some-day — the guy was obviously a communist — and how everything in the world was going to be wonderful. Someday, in the future, in this mythical land. I love speeches like that. All Chekhov's characters do is talk about how the world is going to be better when they get to Moscow, or when they move somewhere else, or when the baby comes, or the new world order comes. It's so sad you could start crying every time you hear it. And so true. People are like that, stupid dreamers. That's what makes them people, I guess. At any rate, I was enjoying the fabulous self-delusion in this partic-ular speech. And when it was over, Judge Face made one of his typically telling comments. He put the book aside, and gently asked, "I wonder where that land is?" He was refer-ring, of course, to the place this poor character was pining for. Chloe didn't miss a beat. She got up, almost stamping her feet, and said, "It's New York."

"What?" I said.

"It's New York. That great fantastical place is New York. Remember? We used to go there? You used to live there?"

"Chloe, what are you talking about?"

"You know what I'm talking about."

"No, I don't."

"Yes, you do, I think you do. Sometimes I feel like I'm in a Chekhov play."

Then she stomped into the bedroom and slammed the door. It was mortifying. If there's one thing I hate, it's couples who argue in public. People get a completely inappropriate glimpse of your personal business, like they're watching you having sex or taking a crap. And the Faces were such nice people. Mrs. Face couldn't handle it, she was morbidly embarrassed. Judge Face is unbelievably tactful, so they passed it all off as a newlyweds' quarrel. He was right. Judge Face was always right. But he was also wrong. It was significant, that little tiff. It wasn't as if Chloe didn't understand the irony — that was the thing about Chloe, she always understood. She knew that New York wasn't the Promised Land, and that hoping and wishing for New York City was the same thing as hoping and wishing for heaven. Or Moscow. She knew all about the Zen idea that you don't have to search for happiness, it's just there, in the woods, beside you. So she knew, as she said, that she *was* in a Chekhov play when she talked about New York that way. She knew she was in a trap. But that didn't mitigate her anger, or our problem.

We argued for a long time afterwards. I thought the best way to deal with everything was to immerse ourselves in the teaching of Paramahansa Yogananda. After all, her yearning for New York was the worldly equivalent of my yearning for her, and maybe there was a way. . . . Maybe if she went to visit now and then or something, she could get it out of her system. She liked to go there to visit her mother, though I'm not so sure that she was a great influence. Chloe hated the woman on one level, for having abandoned her during the war. She was pretentious. If anyone was wrapped up in worldly things, it was Chloe's mom — going for lunches at the Russian Tea Room and hanging out at art galleries. I used to call her "Mother Deah." You get the idea. She was a "deah" sort of person.

I'll have to say that it didn't take a really long time for me to figure out that it wasn't going to work out between Chloe and me. But I don't blame her. I have to give the gal credit, she really was trying.

———

I realize that when I go back and read this, I might come off as a villain. But I won't apologize for taking Chloe away from Radcliffe — it was a horrible place that would have warped her forever. And I don't apologize for loving her and taking her to live with me in the woods. It might seem like I was being hard on a twenty-year-old girl, but I don't see it that way. I don't see myself as a bad man, who does?

No, let me correct that. I'm a very bad man. We're all very bad men and women, that's a universal truth. But I'm also innocent. There's a difference between being bad and being innocent. Even a serial killer, though he's very, very bad, can still be innocent.

———

Have you ever noticed that the best Hitchcock movies are about innocent guys everybody believes are guilty? The exception would be *Shadow of a Doubt*: Joseph Cotten is guilty as sin, but somehow you still care about him. *The 39 Steps* is all about that, and so is *Suspicion*. My favorite of all the innocents everyone thinks is guilty? *Saboteur*. When Priscilla Lane says to Robert Cummings, "You look like a saboteur," you wonder what she means. To me, he just looks like a man. One of my favorite parts of the movie is when Robert Cummings goes into the huge ballroom — as in many of Hitchcock's movies the rich and powerful people are completely corrupt — and the whole thing is being run by traitors. (*The Manchurian Candidate* is stolen from this, actually.) When Cummings yells, "This whole party is a hotbed of spies and saboteurs!" some guy in a fancy tuxedo says, "You're drunk, and you're not even dressed!" This is so true of the world — the one guy who knows the truth doesn't dress as snappily as the utterly deluded jackass. So truth goes unnoticed.

But the best scene of all takes place on a train. Most people don't notice, but Dorothy Parker was one of the film's writers — yet another great artist who turned to drink because of Hollywood. The first time I watched *Saboteur* I noticed her name, and knowing how horrible Hollywood is, I wondered if there'd be a shred of Parker's wit left anywhere. The movie is great, mostly because of Hitchcock, but there is one scene that is particularly acerbic — horribly funny. I'll bet you anything it was written by Dorothy Parker. Cummings and Lane end up looking for refuge on a train. But the train isn't ordinary; it's actually a sleeping car for a circus troupe. They meet the bearded lady, the skeleton man, Siamese twins, a fat lady, and a really irritating midget. These oddballs argue about whether or not to hide Robert and Priscilla from the police, holding a freak's council on the matter. The Siamese twins don't agree, naturally — they're all dolled up like chorus girls and arguing over their newest boyfriend. It's priceless. And when Cummings talks about how few people believe he's innocent, the skeleton man says, "The normal are normally coldhearted." I would bet a million bucks Dorothy Parker wrote that line. What could be closer to the truth? Who shoved the Jews into ovens in Germany? Ordinary folk of the mom-and-pop variety. Who are the most racist assholes in the south? Ordinary country folk, that's who!

The normal are normally coldhearted.

You're damn right they are. Don't fear the psycho killer or the demented recluse who eats nuts and berries and scribbles novels nobody will ever read, fear the nice guy next door, with the car, the suit, and the two-point-five kids. Congratulations, Dorothy, for writing that line. Too bad Hollywood and a few lying, cheating bastard boyfriends conspired to make your life miserable. I'm a guy — I know how horrible guys can be.

———

I've always enjoyed trains. They hold a special, romantic meaning for me, and I'd take them over airplanes any day. One nice thing about them is that you can be alone but with a group of people — a group small enough that it won't make you paranoid. All bets are off, however, if you get seated by some chatty passenger. But most of the time on a train, you can keep your distance from people and still be around them.

These days the kinds of people who take trains are pretty different from the ones who took them back in the fifties. Nowadays trains are for people who are relaxed — if you want to get somewhere in a hurry you take a plane. But back in the fifties trains were still considered speedy — airplanes hadn't quite taken over completely. The reason we ended up on a train was Paramahansa Yogananda's *Autobiography of a Yogi*. We treated it as a marriage textbook, to help us sort out our worldliness issues. In an attempt to cement our relationship, we both wrote to the publishers hoping we might find a guru who could help us to live a holy life in an unholy world.

It turned out that the closest disciple was in Washington D.C., a guy by the name of Swami Premananda. We could go down to Washington and meet him, all we had to do was abstain from eating the day of, and bring some offerings — flowers and money. I was really looking forward to the overnight trip. But when we embarked I realized I was in trouble. Trains have this habit of sexually arousing me. I don't know if it's the continuous vibration, or the intimacy of those little compartments, or if it was having Chloe beside me, practically naked in such a public but private place. On the way down it was all I could do to keep myself from having my way with her, which I'm sure she wouldn't have minded, but it wouldn't really have been appropriate. After all, it was supposed to be a spiritual journey.

Some of that evaporated as soon as we disembarked. It's important to explain a little bit about the neighborhood where the swami's temple was located. It was in a working-class section of our nation's capital. As soon as we got into the taxi, and started going towards the swami's street, Chloe became uncomfortable. Why? Well, the area was pretty seedy, pretty basic. You know, rundown little shopping areas, closed stores and peeling paint, little shoeless children, and old men pushing shopping carts with their drunken friends passed out in them. When we got to the swami's, she was even worse. The temple was located in a storefront — the downstairs of an old house. It was cheap-looking and it had been reconverted in a bad way, with low, stained ceilings. That was one of the first things that Chloe noticed when we got there. While we were waiting for the swami she said, "The ceilings."

So I said, "What about them?"

"They're so low."

I didn't understand what all the fuss was about, it didn't bother me. I shrugged and she pointed to a table that was between the little rickety card-table chairs we were sitting on. It had a lace tablecloth and was covered with photographs of family and, I guess, other yogis.

"Photographs." she said, pointing to the table.

"So?"

She repeated the word again, with gossipy disgust. "Photographs."

We had reached a class divide. But it all related, ultimately, to spirituality. When we met the swami, he was a nice guy. He gave us each a mantra, and taught us how to raise breath and watch it. The breathing exercises were relaxing, you really felt like you were in another world. This was exactly why we came; it really did the trick. But Chloe was offended because the swami's place was in a working-class neighborhood. And like the homes of a lot of lower-class people, the swami's had low ceilings and tacky, sentimental family photographs on the table. Her reaction made me mad. So what if the swami wasn't brought up in the best of families?

It was exactly like the scene in *Saboteur* where nobody will listen to Robert Cummings because he's not wearing a fancy suit. And there was Chloe, whose parents were cosmopolitan and had traveled the world . . . whose father knew a Fra Angelico from a da Vinci *Virgin and Child* — I'm improvising like a goddamn jazz musician, right now, this pisses me off so much — but wouldn't have known the Godhead if he tripped over it. So it pissed me off to see her get all upset because her spiritual advisor didn't have good taste. Now, I can't claim to come from humble origins, as I told you, my father was successful in meat packing and I never had to complain. But I know snobbery when I see it. I felt betrayed. When Chloe realized I was angry, she tried to pretend that she wasn't acting la-di-da, but it was too late.

To make matters worse, she was quite charming on the way back on the train. As usual, she wanted to make things right, so she chose to get much too excited — hysterical actually — about finding her third eye. The swami had told us that if we did our breathing exercises consistently, we might begin to see a white light in the middle of our foreheads. If we did, we were developing a third eye. Chloe smuggled a little bottle of alcohol onto the train, and we each had a swig. I know we shouldn't have, but it was a celebration. We started giggling and flirting, and Chloe went on and on about the third eye, and how excited she would be if she got one. I found it both bizarre and annoying. She was treating the whole third eye thing materialistically, as if it were a new outfit, or a trendy handbag. I must admit — despite my disgust — we made love on the train that night. It was sad. I think I was sort of saying goodbye to Chloe. I guess I figured we'd probably never make love again, at least not like before, because, not only was she having difficulty renouncing things, her attitude toward the swami was so offensive. It was upsetting, and I dealt with the whole thing badly. A part of me still loved her, but deep inside I realized that it was never going to work.

We conceived our first child that night. Nine months later, to the day, Chloe gave birth to our little girl.

———

I have to admit, it was odd watching Chloe become pregnant. She was always beautiful, but the fact that she ceased to be as physically attractive to me — for a while at least — was a good thing. I was able to live with her without having to struggle with physical desire. But once the baby was born there was no competition. How could I be in love with Chloe when I had this little girl? The thing I had loved so much in Chloe, her innocence, the baby had in spades. And I didn't have to worry about the baby ignoring the Godhead or being swamped in pretensions. Babies are godly. They live in the now and know the truth about things — that the world is a beautiful place that you want to explore forever.

Chloe couldn't help but notice that I loved the baby more than her. And that made her resent me more. The only time I can remember — in the next six years that we lived in the same house together — that we actually had fun again, iron-ically, was on a trip to New York.

Why did I stay with her for that long, if I knew it was over coming back from Washington on the train?

Why does anybody do anything?

People are stubborn and I'm no exception. If you've made a bad life choice you don't want to say so, because then you'll have to admit wasting years of your life. If Chloe wasn't the right woman for me, why had I been stupid enough to choose her? What does that say about me and my judgment? You have to realize that people are, generally, of little importance to me. All I need is my writing.

I don't know if I've truly explained what writing a book is like. You travel to another world. It seems more real, and all the people in it seem more real than the ones in real life. And since you've made up a world that you'd like to live in, it can be hard to leave, even for a minute, and connect with the so-called real world. I'm sure this was even the case with people who wrote nightmarish books, people like Kafka and Dostoevsky. I think people are always writing about places they would rather be, it's just that with those who are truly demented, the places that they'd like to be still seem like nightmares to "normal" people. Some people want to live in a nightmare; I don't see any point in criticizing that. More power to them.

I'm sure psychiatrists would criticize me for preferring fantasy to reality. So what? It works for me. Let's face it, what was Freud most famous for? Analyzing dreams. When it comes down to it, Freud was simply another Section Man, another academic. Is nothing sacred? Dreams were meant to be dreamt, not analyzed. They are not real — that's the point. If reality is lousy, why shouldn't you escape? I guess you can tell what I'm getting at here. I think that the world art creates is holy. It's a place that, once you enter, has as much validity as the other world. I remember watching the Fourth of July fireworks when I was young, wondering what it would be like to live in them. A psychiatrist would say, "He obviously wants to escape his horrific family." Okay, sure. But that's not the point. The point is that I wanted to live inside the fireworks. I didn't have any idea what it would be like to live in a rocket, but I had a great old time wondering about it — when I was a kid, I wanted to write a book called *The Firecracker People*.

I'm not going to pretend that it was any bed of roses for Chloe living with someone most people would call a lunatic living for his art. Soon after were married, I built a little study for myself out of an old shack down the path from the house. It was my own little bunker — with a view. It got me away from the wife and the kids, and I could go off into my own little world. I know this drove Chloe nearly crazy eventually, which is why she saw a psychiatrist for a while in Springfield. I didn't want her to go.

I think what finally set her off was the pee incident. And also the orgone box.

When my daughter was born, I got into types of healing Chloe didn't seem to understand. I resented that. She didn't even make an effort.

Okay, I know the things I'm about to talk about might sound wacky, especially to someone who's never heard of them. It's times like this when I wish you were sitting in front of me, that I could see the expression on your face, see how you react. I read a fascinating essay in a homeopathic journal about the beneficial effects of drinking your own urine. I know it sounds strange, even disgusting, but a lot of revolutionary ideas often do. It has to do with a homeopathic principle: that all medicines are poisons. Most doctors don't know this. The best medicines are those that, in higher doses, will kill you. I know most doctors aren't aware of this because they have such a terrible time treating cancer. One reason is because they start out with such high doses. Doctors are intimately linked to drug companies, which are like all other businesses listed on the stock market. In the case of cancer — and I'm sure lots of other diseases as well — doctors prescribe treatments in massive quantities, in order to drive up the profits of pharmaceutical companies. You'll notice that birth control pills and cancer drugs were initially prescribed in doses that were much too high, until patients started dying. The protests forced physicians to prescribe much safer dosages.

The benefits of drinking your own urine are widely known. Gandhi did it when he was fasting. It purifies your own system in much the way any poison does in small doses. Drinking your own urine has cured people of cancer. It was necessary for me to pee at night, let the pee sit, and then drink it in the morning, first thing. This means that there was a "pee jar" beside our bed. Chloe found this unappealing for obvious reasons, especially after she got up once in the night and knocked the jar over. Finally she said, "Either the pee jar goes, or I go." So I gave up the whole before-bed peeing thing. Instead I peed in the morning and kept the dose by my desk to drink at night. It was less convenient, and very annoying.

The orgone box was even more of an issue. I think it's because when I was working, even though I told her I could not be disturbed under any circumstances, she still insisted on disturbing me now and then. The power dynamic was weird. It became all about whether or not Chloe had the right to interfere with my private, creative, spiritual space. The orgone box became a symbol of my need for privacy.

What's an orgone box? The design is pretty simple, wood on the outside and metal on the inside. It was developed by Wilhelm Reich, who was a pretty interesting character. Reich was a Viennese psychologist and a contemporary of Freud — but he eventually broke with "The Master." This made sense because Reich was on a far more interesting track: more practical, less academic. It's interesting that his experiments got him into so much trouble with the Nazis that he had to flee Europe. But then he moved to the United States and, funnily enough, things weren't much better. Reich's theories on the importance of sex and sexuality proved a bit too controversial for our government. In 1957, all of Reich's books and papers were seized and burned. He was placed in prison, where he died. Does that say something about the kind of people who run this country? I discovered his box just before all this happened. For a while, before bad weather destroyed it, I had in my possession something that was technically considered illegal, obscene even.

Reich thought that the most important energy in the world was something he called the life force, which was depleted and then replenished in the sexual act — during orgasm. He believed that human beings need orgasms. This made sense to me because, try as I might to rid myself of the need for sexual release, I couldn't make it work. The orgone box — big enough for a person to sit in — was designed to attract the orgone energy through the wooden material, which was then conducted by the metal into the box. Essentially what you'd do was sit in the box for hours on end, the longer the better. You could tell it was working because it would get very hot inside.

The box was the perfect place for me. I loved it in there. I was completely alone and no one could bother me. It was great for meditating. In a way, the whole box resembled an outhouse, the difference being that there was no stink, and you could justify staying in there longer. I used to claim that I couldn't hear if anyone was banging on it. This used to infuriate Chloe. I think somewhere inside she knew that I could hear her. I can't tell you what satisfaction it gave me to sit inside that box with Chloe yelling at me from outside. Then I'd blithely appear, hours later, and ask, "Oh, were you calling me?"

It drove her nuts.

Thank God we got rid of the damn box before Chloe tried to burn down the house. That's another story.

before she tried to burn down the house. She was seeing her psychiatrist in New York once a month. This guy was committed to the idea of people realizing their potential, realizing who they really were and what they wanted. Chloe would come back from one of these sessions ranting and raving about how she had to express herself, and how I was trapping her, making her live a life that she hated. Right. She made the choice to live in the woods with me, and she also chose to get me drunk, twice, and we ended up with two kids. There was no way I was moving to the city. I hated cities, and besides, the story I had written about Chloe had been quite successful — phenomenally so, it was even more successful than my novel — which made it dangerous for me to go anywhere in public. I'd be mobbed if people figured out who I was, it was really that bad. To me, it was an indication of Chloe's selfishness, that she might think I could bear to be anywhere near people under these circumstances.

That's what we owe the generation of therapists. Back then, it was all about self-realization; now it's all about victimhood. The same thing, really. Endless solipsism. Okay, sure, I guess I'm a little solipsistic myself. But mine is a *moral* solipsism, and that's different. My self-obsession is not simply vanity; in fact, I do everything I can to *not* make it about that. Instead, I'm examining my motives constantly to discover a purity of being and acting. That's different than worrying about whether or not you have "realized" yourself — which leads to photography and macramé, among other things. So I generally didn't enjoy these little outings to the therapist in the city, but since I knew we had to go there, I also knew that it would be a good time to schedule a dinner with my British publisher.

This guy was one of the most infuriating clods I'd ever had to deal with. He was intensely excitable, in general, but it was his literary enthusiasm that really bugged me. He was a failed author, of course, being kept by a rich, older woman in London. He wasn't much of a catch though, with his cloying baby fat and dyed blond hair. He was arty, and prone to dropping names — for some reason he insisted on talking about famous literary types around me. As if all of us writers were part of some big, happy, literary family. Only dullards like him are friends with tons of authors. Most authors aren't friends with each other, they are merely compelled, usually out of necessity, to have an occasional drink with shallow people like him, people who say things like, "Oh I was talking to Brendan Behan the other day." And sure, you're human, you can't help but wonder what Brendan Behan might be thinking or saying — but then the thought of this idiot running to Brendan Behan and telling him what *you* are thinking or saying is enough to shut any respectable author up in mid-sentence. And then there was his shocking inability to understand what I was doing with my work. When my first book was about to be published in the U.K. he asked, "Does this novel have a definitive attitude towards juvenile delinquency?" It was really funny. Actually, it was a last-ditch attempt to get me to encapsulate the whole thing. Imagine stepping onto an airplane and asking the stewardess, "Oh, by the way, does this thing have any fuel?" As if the most important thing of all was an afterthought. Jeez, I didn't want to dignify his stupidity. Of course not, no novel worth its salt has a definitive attitude towards juvenile delinquency. Secretly,

sure, I love juvenile delinquents. I always loved Marlon
Brando, everything he did. He was a much better delinquent
than Paul Newman, who was a bit too blue-eyed for me.
When it comes to my kids, it's another story. I would rather
that didn't happen to them. But as for the novel, it's just a fantasy. It doesn't have an opinion about anything. But this guy's
a publisher, so you shouldn't have to try to explain good writing to him.

I figured that if I was going to leave my orgone box and
pee jar, my meditation and writing, my macrobiotic diet and
gorgeous view, and hightail it to the big city, I might as well
do two horrible things at once: give my wife another little jolt
of self-involvement, and have a drink with the most horrible
man in the world. If you're going to have a bad weekend,
why not go all the way?

The restaurant was toney, the waiters all homosexuals. I
don't say that because I've got anything against homosexuals.
But like anything, in large doses, they can be a bit hard to
take. It was the kind of place where the flowers have to be just
right, and everyone rushes around catering to your every need
because they think this means you'll come back again and
again to be pampered. I hate this type of place. Give me a
greasy spoon, with a wispy little waitress who tries to keep the
old men entertained with stories about rice pudding, any day.
Eating is loathsome. At best, pragmatic. Like sex. Why make
a big deal out of it? But I'm human, and when I'm tempted, I
end up eating something I shouldn't. I ordered snails dripping
in garlic butter. I can't tell you what food like that does in your
stomach. It congeals into a hard substance that sticks to the
walls of your intestines. It's almost impossible to expel. But

it's also tasty. I've developed the habit of throwing up if I find myself in a situation where I can't help indulging. I just put my finger down my throat and that does the trick. What's the point of letting that garbage sit when you won't even be able to digest it?

You can imagine how much I was looking forward to the meal. The editor wanted to discuss the book's cover. It was a shady deal. I'd laid down the law long before: my books were to have nothing on their covers besides the title and my name. You can never trust an artist to come up with something appropriate. And even if they do, it spoils the book for the reader. The whole point of literature is that it's supposed to set your imagination racing so you can envision what characters look like. All that gets tossed into the garbage when a publisher supplies a flashy little picture of the hero in his favorite cap or the heroine in her prettiest blue dress. When this guy called to say he wanted to discuss the cover, I tried to make my position clear. But he insisted. "We really have to talk about it over dinner." God, he was so pushy.

I should probably explain something about myself, something you would have no way of knowing. I'm letting my hair down here, telling the truth in all its blemished glory. I'm a pretty nice guy. No, really. I am. I'm not saying I'm nice deep down. That would be vain — and a lie. I'm saying that I *appear*, to most people, to be nice. I do. As I say, I'm pretty good-looking, in a tall, slender, dark, gangly sort of way. And because most people are so superficial that goes miles towards getting their sympathy. On top of that, I try to please people. I want everyone to be happy. It's something the critics complain about with my writing, they say it's much too entertaining. Life is short, and painful, and then you die. So why not try to make things a little easier? Mostly, I hate confrontation. And since I hate people in general, and all their vain little manipulations and control games, I would probably be getting into about ten confrontations a minute if I followed my inner instincts. So I smile a lot, and even manage to laugh, and turn on the charm, when pressed. Anyway, I wanted you to know that I do appear to be a much nicer guy than I am, and I'm aware of it. That's how I keep people in the dark about my true nature, my real feelings.

Well, this guy's pathetic manipulations impressed me, in a sick way. He wanted to take me out to dinner, have some wine and some snails, you know, oil me up so he could put his knife in slick and easy. There would barely be a pop when it broke the skin. I thought it was amusing actually, that he would think that dinner in a jazzy restaurant would ease the pain. Like he had worked everything out. He was also tiptoeing around, which I hate, treating me like a bomb about to explode. Even though I'm charming as hell, generally, I *had* gone off once or twice in front of him. That's my pattern, nice as can be until it's time to explode. And so there was lots of attention being paid to my "needs," and preparatory statements like, "We'd like to sit down and talk, to make sure we hear all your preferences before we go ahead with the next step."

Yeah, right.

After I put down the phone, keeping my cool, I complained to Chloe about having to go. She sweetly suggested that she had to go see her therapist anyway, so why didn't she come along, and maybe bring along her little modeling friend, Delilah, to ease the pain. I had met Delilah once or twice and she wasn't my type, a bit too worldly for my taste, but she certainly was a dish. She was well turned out, skinny, the way models are, blond, and dressed in all the latest styles. All this gave me a great idea. Why didn't the two of them come along, sit at another table, pretend to be hookers, and then, at a prearranged moment, I'd invite them over and we'd have a little fun.

Chloe went crazy for the idea. A little too crazy, as far as I was concerned. Sure, I thought it would be fun, but I was doing it for practical reasons, to ease the pain of meeting with a money-grabbing, lying, cheating dotard. For her, it was a party game. There was also something about the scheme that fed my male vanity. Not a good thing. I knew that my wife and her friend were certainly young enough to fool this guy, who would never for a minute imagine I was married to one of these gorgeous girls. But, I have to admit, it was touching the way Chloe got all excited about the idea of us pulling the wool over somebody's eyes, and having fun at the same time.

The plan was simple. I'd meet the publisher at the restaurant. Chloe and Delilah would turn up soon after we arrived and sit nearby. I would flirt with Chloe all through the meal, she would flirt back. At the perfect moment, I would invite them over, and our little playlet would begin. I knew Chloe would be great at this; her best thing was improvising outrageous situations.

It all worked out perfectly and was a lot of fun. The greasy publisher was true to form. I can barely explain how horrible he was. What had happened was that the paperback version of my novel had already appeared in London, and — are you ready for this? — *by mistake*, yes, *by mistake* — someone

(apparently not my publisher, some hapless underling) had put
a tasteless image on the cover, a photograph that sounded far
too much like it was from the movie *The Graduate*. (This was
way before *The Graduate* though.) There was an older woman
dressed in garters and stockings, tempting a young man. All
this had nothing at all to do with my novel, which featured no
older women at all. I crammed delicious indigestible snails
down my throat as I digested the news. Apparently, there was
nothing that could be done . . . *"fait accompli . . ."* nobody's
fault really. It never is. He knew my position, but the publisher
wanted to prepare me, to soften the blow. And he was certain,
because he knew of my great "generosity and understanding,"
that I would forgive him for what was, in the grand scheme of
things, a "little problem." It was a great book anyway, perhaps
one of the greatest. So why worry? As if I would be charmed
by this half-wit's clumsy compliments. The more he talked
about why nothing could be done about this "minor mishap,"
the more I flirted with Chloe and Delilah. Jesus, they looked
fabulous. They almost cheered me up. It was a little frightening, actually, how convincing they were. Both wore too much
makeup. Chloe, being truly witty deep down, had gone for the
sad hooker thing. She'd even ripped her nylons a little bit and
had found a sequined purse. Delilah was perfectly tasteful, and
stunning in the clothes department, but she was wearing her
hair up in a bizarre way. So, as the publisher offered one more
little excuse, I leaned over the table conspiratorially and said,
"Have a look at them."

"Who?"

"Those gals at that table over there. How could you miss
them?"

"You've been in the country too long."

"Why do you say that?"

"It's pretty obvious, they're hookers."

"I know what they are."

"They only want one thing."

"You think?"

I could tell that my new, unexpected penchant for ladies of the evening had unsettled him. I guess he figured all along he had used the wrong approach. Wining and dining was, after all, not my vice: if he'd set me up with a little party girl in the first place maybe I'd be putty in his hands. But seeing as I had moved to the country and had strict rules about everything — editors, and book covers, and publicity, for instance — I think he found it odd that I was a professional sleazebag. When I felt like I couldn't take his bilge for one more moment I said, "Let's invite them over."

"Who?"

"The hookers. Who else?"

"Do you . . . Do you really want to?"

"Why the hell not?"

"Well, sure . . . I guess so."

It was great to watch him squirm. The joint was so fancy that Chloe and Delilah looked completely out of place. I'm surprised the management hadn't tossed them out. The key was they didn't look appalling, just over the top. We asked the waiter if he could get the nice ladies a couple of chairs. The waiter was pleasant. But his "Certainly, sir!" added to the general smarminess, the "We'll do anything to make the customer happy, even help them pick up hookers" atmosphere of the establishment. Delilah made a play for the publisher, and Chloe made a play for me. I almost lost it when she joked, "You know what they say about tall men?"

"No," I said, acting innocent.

"Tall feet!"

She had a great hooker laugh — it was much too loud, and went on and on, so you wanted to kick her, to put her, and everyone else, out of their misery. Delilah was perfect too, very practical. She kept asking the fat publisher how much money he made, and when he told her, she asked him if he was carrying a lot of money with him. It was like she was going to roll him or something. I'd told Chloe about his horrible, dyed blond hair, which had obviously surpassed her expectations. Now and then, she'd stop chewing her gum — she was chewing gum *and* drinking wine, it was classic — and yell across the table, "Is your hair real?" It really irritated him. "Are you sure it's real?" He told her yes. So then, a few minutes later: "But, yeah, but is that the real *color*?" After a while the publisher finally got horny. Unbeknownst to me, Delilah had been playing footsie with him. It was time to make his day.

I stood up and said. "I've had enough of this. Come on, Chloe, Delilah." I had one hooker on each arm now. "Listen, it's about time I hightailed it out of this joint and got a real taste of the city. And oh yeah, one more thing, I'm going to sue the pants off you, buddy, over this 'minor mishap.' See ya later." And with that, we were off — lots of giggling and tripping, quite a scene.

I'm telling you all this because I want you to know how much fun Chloe and I could have, why I loved her so much. The truth was, this was the kind of life she wanted all the time, going to fancy restaurants and pulling pranks. But for me the kick was in humiliating a confirmed creep. I'll have to admit that I couldn't help being critical of her performance. As perfect and hilarious as it was — touching even — it was a little bit condescending. Chloe could have played a classy hooker, but instead she chose to play a girl who had obviously gotten her start on the streets. It smacked of class snobbery again.

The more Chloe saw her shrink, the more she began to long for outings like this. She wanted to go back to Radcliffe to "realize" herself, she wanted to work, and she wanted to have a life of her own. All of which was completely opposite to what I wanted. She had two kids now anyway, and the youngest one was still practically a baby. The next couple of years we gradually moved apart. I'll have to admit we were both pretty civil about it, and it happened slowly.

Was I broken up about it? Sure I was. But as I said, it happened so slowly, and I was so tired of fighting with her, I don't think I could say that I was noticeably sad. What did happen was that for the five or six years after we split, I began to get incredibly lonely.

Yeah, me. Lonely.

———

Okay, so I hated the world but still needed someone around. For a while, the children helped. My daughter, especially. But as much as I would get lost in the reverie of our little walks, hypnotized by her absolutely pure, innocent, yet unfettered curiosity, I wasn't so stupid that I'd forget she would grow up and lose most of that incredibly focused, egoless sense of play. I never imagined she would stay a child, but it was disappointing to watch her develop an ego, an attachment to the world. I tried to stop it, but that was impossible, since we still had a TV, and watched old movies together. And then there was Chloe, who insisted on introducing the children to the outside world. She thought it would be healthy for them. God knows why.

With my son, it was and is different. I can't say I adore him any less, but a father's bond with his little girl is special. I've never been a guy's guy — a man's man. This wasn't helpful during the two years I spent in the Army. I can't really do anything handy, which is why I immediately applied to be an officer. I can do garden things, and household chores, and, if pressed, chop wood, but I'm not really a fix-it sort of person. Sports? They remind me of prep school. God, the last thing I wanted for my boy was for him to be one of those sporty guys, who's always trying to get you to root for this team or that one. I'm not deluded though, I realized that he had to be whatever he wanted. Almost to spite me, it seemed, both kids became athletic. I found it sort of sweet in my daughter; with my son it was too predictable, even a little frightening. Over the years I wound up taking him to endless football games. You can imagine how horrible that was. But it shows how much I loved him.

What was really happening during the failure of my marriage was that I was beginning to think that there were no landsmen for me.

Landsmen. I should explain the word. When Jewish settlers first came to the New World, they formed societies dedicated to helping immigrants. They were kind of like community centers, but they were also more, giving people financial help and emotional support. Landsmen made you feel that you belonged.

For me, being in this world is like being in a foreign country. I've spent most of my life searching for lonely "immigrants" who, like me, don't really fit in — people who might understand me. It's not so much that they'll understand my problems, or respond to my needs, like some goddamn psychiatric self-help book, but that they might be kindred spirits. I thought I had found this in Chloe, but ultimately I couldn't have been more wrong. Judge Face was something of a landsman. But he died a few years after we met, and he was a man. Men don't make good landsmen for me. I don't really know how to bond with guys. At some point, most guys act like idiots, making some crude remark, being competitive, or punching me on the arm, saying, "You know what I mean, fella?" I hate that stuff. I've never met a man I really liked, except in my fiction. I keep thinking I'll meet female landsmen. I'm not going to say that women are more instinctual, because that's crap, and I know most women don't like to hear it. I think it's just that they're willing to be vulnerable and honest. Men never really let their guard down with other men. Women let their guard down all the time, which is what makes them charming and, ultimately, sexy. It's also what gets you into trouble. The problem is that when you get to know anyone — man or woman — you run the risk of peeling away all the layers until you get to the mushy center. For me, the mushy center is this: they're doing everything to please you, to make you happy. I don't want that. Jesus, isn't it possible to meet someone who is a natural landsman? Who sincerely happens to like the same things I do, who thinks the same way? Why do people always have to try to please you? You discover that they've been lying, and your hopes and dreams are shattered.

By the time Chloe and I decided to get an actual legal divorce, a short story appeared in the *New Yorker* that proved to be my final publication. I know I've gone on about critics, but this marked the ultimate betrayal. I put everything into the story, everything. I had committed myself to writing about this family. I had really burrowed into the head of one of the kids, the most important kid, and I thought I knew exactly what made him tick. It was like my novel, in the sense that I really liked this guy and identified with him — even though he was only twelve. He charmed the hell out of me, and I couldn't see why he wouldn't charm the hell out of everyone else too.

The opposite happened. I don't mean with the public. The public bought the thing like it was going out of style, mainly because I hadn't published anything in years. But the critics went nuts. It was embarrassing how vindictive they were: "Yet another slim offering that doesn't justify publication." And: "So self-indulgent, he's lost his old touch." First, they've got your old work for comparison, and they can't believe you'd do something different. And this was definitely different, even though they all claimed it was the same. They also called it old-fashioned — out of style. Just because my writing still had meaning, because it was funny. And yes, damn it, because it was touching. You can't be touching these days. It's enough to make me want to write something about the Second World War — which I would never do, now, even though I experienced it in spades. I did write some things about the war, both during and after, but I'm not sure about that stuff. There's no way to do justice to that kind of horror. Now I'm sort of ashamed that I even tried. But it's that kind of writing, that "the horror of the world has left me speechless" genre, which is so popular these days. It all started with Joseph Conrad, God love him. Started and stopped as far as I'm concerned. The horror of the world has the opposite effect on me, it makes me want to talk your ear off, brother, and I don't see why *that* response is any more valid than silence.

At least it shouldn't be.

So, the reaction to my story deeply discouraged me. With what happened with Chloe, and then this publication, I felt like I could no longer reach anyone. I would still talk to Chloe, and she could still be supportive now and then, God bless her. When I complained about the critics she said: "That's some stupid reviewer. Thousands are buying it, why don't you think about them?" She was right. Why should I care what the critics said when people — real people — were buying my books? But I never meet them; I never hear what they say. Except when they write me letters. And they do write thousands of them. And okay, I read every one, searching for a landsman. And now and then I actually respond, but only when the letter seems to be coming from someone truly intelligent. But I've had some bad experiences with that too. One woman I responded to started stalking me. I had to call the police. She actually moved to a town nearby and started hanging out at the end of my driveway. Here I am, looking for a kindred spirit, and I get a certifiable nut. Right or wrong, elitist or not, I have to be honest; reviewers affect me. And the reviews for that story made me so angry that I decided to give up. Forever.

I don't mean writing. Just publishing.

I know that sounds crazy too, crazier than a pee jar or an orgone box. But think about it. Since I couldn't detach myself from reviewers — the stupid, fatuous crap they spew to feed their own egos — there was nothing to do but abandon the act of putting my work before them. I realized that publishing was completely materialistic, anyway. There's nothing you can do about that. Even if you don't care about the money (most writers don't make any, and I'd already made all I needed) if you're publishing, you're trying to get a response, to be validated, to be a part of the world of reviews, and talk shows, and photographs in the paper, and speculation about your goddamn meaningless personal life. Isn't writing about communication? Isn't the point that you want to communicate with people, deliver a message, a feeling, a sense of life? There's no denying it. So I figured I'd put my writing away in a fireproof safe somewhere, lock it up. If it was found, it was meant to be found. Here I am talking about Zen all the time, about being one with the universe. How hypocritical would I be if I didn't trust the universe to know whether my work was meant to be read?

You're reading this now, right?

You must be.

Please say you are.

———

When I stopped thinking about publishing, I finally began to truly think about writing. Before, every time I sat down to write a new story I had to go through the process of pushing out of my mind every review, every response, everything from the world that threatened to intrude and ruin it. Writing became much easier when I didn't have to do that, because as far as I was concerned, no one was going to read my work, except God. And believe it or not, God is very forgiving.

So it was all the more ironic that the next important person in my life, the next prospective landsman, the next girl who stole my heart, was also a writer.

But maybe that's not strange at all.

My daily ritual is strict, and mostly involves writing, meditating, and eating properly. Two days a week, however, I allow myself a break. Perhaps break isn't the right word. I don't see it as a pleasure or as a release. More a duty. You see, the things most people see as a duty — writing, and meditating, and eating well — are things I feel compelled to do. But I know I should have *some* contact with the outside world, even if it's going to the post office or reading the Sunday New York Times. I approach these tasks with trepidation. I have to prepare myself. What sort of ogres will I meet or read about? Will my disgust for the world make me so depressed that I won't be able to go back to my work? Will I be brutally hurt?

I am, usually. Even by articles that don't concern me.

It was in the newspaper that I found her. She was a precocious eighteen year old, and she'd written an autobiographical piece for the *New York Times Magazine*. Her picture was on the cover. I always ready myself for the worst — gird myself for the onslaught. But nothing could have prepared me for this.

When I saw her photograph, it was as if someone had shot me, or punched me in the gut. I think that says something about love right there. You'd think it would be a good feeling, but it's usually traumatic, painful, a shock — even in the first instance.

She was sitting on the floor of what looked like a library. The setting got to me right away. Surrounded by books, and sitting. That's the proper way to be with books, of course, humble before them. She was leaning slightly to one side, with her arm on a low bookshelf, supporting her head. Her whole body was tilted. One hand — she had very long fingers for a girl — was supporting her head. The other was curled charmingly around her shoe. Something a little girl might do. She was wearing a sweater, jeans, and sneakers, and had long brown hair. But there was something about her expression.

The only way to describe it would be rueful. Like when you see a baby that looks older than its years. I saw a baby like that once around here. The woman and her kid were performing, you know, the way some parents and their children do. But the kid was innocent; it was the adult who was making a big deal about everything. I was waiting behind the two of them in the post office. The woman went on and on in a loud voice. Then she would look back at me as if to say, "Isn't my little girl precious?" The kid was precious, there was no denying it. But the mother's attitude was nauseating. I love my children, but when I take them out in public, I keep it low-key. I don't "perform" my relationship with them so

that everyone sees how much I love them. I figure if a parent
has to do that in public, then God knows what they do to the
kid at home. Anyway, this baby was taking it pretty well —
she was still practically a baby, in a stroller — and she wore
a remarkable expression. She looked like she was about a
hundred years old, even though she was barely two. The fur-
rowed brow, the wrinkles around the mouth, and the eyes,
everything. She was elfin — not in a cute way, in a knowing
way. Christ, it was like she was a goddamn seer. The wisdom
of the ages was in that face. She obviously knew a hell of a
lot more than her mother, and I couldn't help thinking she
was fundamentally embarrassed by her parent. I know that
sounds odd, but I do think it's possible for kids to feel embar-
rassment in a basic sort of way. I don't mean she was angry at
her mother or putting her down. On the contrary, she was
putting up with her mother. Which was so damn big of her.
The kid's expression was rueful. "See what I have to endure?"
Since her mother was going to burst a blood vessel if I didn't
acknowledge her amazing child, I did. I said, "Quite a daughter you've got there."

"Oh yes," said Mummy. "We love her very much. She's
changed our lives."

Right there I wanted to take out a gun and shoot her. Gee,
I would love to say my kids have changed my life, but the fact
is, they haven't. I wish I could say they made me into a perfect person, but that would be a lie. I'm still the same
screwed-up guy I was before I had them. And as I said, the
problem with kids is that they grow up. This is an idea that
women like this are obviously not familiar with. God help the
child — God bless the child for Christ's sake — who's got a

beatified mother, so spiritually undeveloped she thinks a child can bring her to nirvana.

I didn't say any of this — I'm not that horrible — but I couldn't help making an observation. "She looks wise," I said.

"Oh yes," said Mummy, "She is. She's taught us so much."

Another cliché. Jesus, they were pouring out of her like water from a tap. I decided to stop things right there. "Actually she looks kind of old."

"Oh, you think so?"

"She looks a little bit like an old man," I said, and then, to keep up the admiration, I added, "She's amazing."

"Yes, she is," sighed Mummy. "She truly is."

But I wouldn't let up. "She looks really old," I said, hunkering down and looking at the wizened old baby in the carriage. "It's almost eerie."

"I suppose it is out of the ordinary," she said.

Then I put in one more for good measure. "I can't believe how old she looks."

"Please stop saying that," said Mummy. She was clearly disturbed by my comments, so I stood up and left them alone. I got myself out of that one. Mummy was looking at me like I was weird. I suppose I am, but I think she was weirder.

Daphne's expression in the photograph was a lot like the one on that kid. She had to put up with a lot, she had endured a lot. But she wasn't complaining about it, she wasn't whining, or acting depressed. She was sort of shrugging, but not in an irresponsible way. Saying, "Heck, that's the way it is. There's nothing I can do about it."

It was a very Zen expression.

That picture made a lasting impression, but another had

an even deeper effect. There were lots of photos of her at various high school events, and one of them was taken at a dance. It was a costume party, and all the kids were dressed up. Usually, at these shindigs, people wear something romantic and/or sexy, or at least flattering. Not Daphne. She was dressed like Minnie Mouse. *Minnie Mouse.* There was no one anywhere near her. She was completely alone, looking as forlorn as you could look dressed like a cheery cartoon character. That picture said it all. Everyone costumed as princes and princesses, and Daphne looking like a mouse's wife.

I don't want you to get the idea that all I did was look at the photos. The pictures were the first thing I saw, and so I'll always remember them. But I remember the article too. It was honest. Hell, I could have written the damn thing at her age. The main theme of it was that she didn't fit in. It was the era of The Beatles, and women's liberation, and the times they were a-changing, and there she was in the center — at the calm of the storm. I don't mean she was old-fashioned. She discussed things like abortion, and women's rights, and everything. But her opinions were not always consistent — something I truly respect. They seemed to be her *own* opinions. She seemed completely unfazed about — and, in fact, detached from — the fads and crazes, the marches and protests that were swirling around her. It was so trendy then to be a young revolutionary. But it was completely clear from this article that instead she was just being herself, in the face of tremendous pressure to join. It was clear to me that she was totally alone, not a joiner at all. She was at sea, but not adrift — she knew where she was going. She wanted to be a writer, and she was damn good at it.

I was profoundly excited.

I agonized over it for a while. I'm prepared for most things I read — huge praise for bad books, analysis of the latest trends, dishonest politicians, and vacuous gossip. But I wasn't prepared for this. I wasn't prepared to fall in love with a newspaper article.

Of course I wanted to write to her. The piece was a thinly disguised plea — not just between the lines, between the lines she was obviously lonely — a kind of open letter. She was an outcast and a kindred spirit. Maybe even a landsman.

I'd never written a letter to a famous person before — except one to Ernest Hemingway, in Paris, during the war . . . but that's another story. Lots of people had written letters to me. I knew that the first thing was to can the bull — not to over-compliment her, or seem like an acolyte. I certainly didn't want to appear sleazy. My motives were not crass. Yes, I found her beautiful. She wasn't conventionally pretty like Chloe, but that didn't mean I wasn't attracted. Still, physical attraction was the last thing on my mind.

I know you might not believe me. But in fact, I convinced myself it would be a good idea to write to her — for two reasons. First, she was already famous, in her own way, and she might understand what it was like to be like me, even on the smallest scale. I was sure she would get tons of responses to her article. It would be a tough job plowing through them. I knew that if she was at all like me she would hope desperately that somewhere in those letters was a voice that would resonate. Secondly, I was pretty sure my motive was absolutely pure — I was, after all, writing her to put an end to my insufferable loneliness. I didn't think I would develop sexual feelings. I wouldn't have wanted anything to ruin the possibility of a friendship. The opportunity for one was simply too tempting.

I labored over that letter the way I do over any piece of writing. It had to be completely honest, and it had to be expressed in the simplest, most immediate terms. And it had to be accurate. I told her that I identified with her situation, that I had been young once, and unable to fit in. I said — without flattery — that I thought she was talented, and had seen a lot of life for someone of her tender years. I also hinted at the dangers that might be lurking out there for someone blessed with her talent and innocence.

The letter I received in return was more than I ever could have hoped for. The article in *The Times* was more formal — even the best newspapers have a house style that is somewhat restrictive. Her letters, on the other hand, were spontaneous, unrestrained, even slightly incomprehensible. But when she wasn't explaining herself clearly, she knew it, and apologized. She wore her heart on her sleeve. This is probably one of my most important requirements in friends. If I detect the tiniest trace of deception or hypocrisy, I reject them.

She talked a lot in her letters about the play she was in — Shakespeare's *Measure for Measure*. This was another way that we were alike. We were both attracted to the theater. I say attracted because I could tell that, like me, she wasn't cut out for it. It's hard for people like us. I could tell — from the picture and her letters — that she was damn charming. And being damn charming isn't easy: people want to put you into plays or movies, and if you're good-looking, or even interesting-looking, sometimes they won't let up. This should be a compliment, and it is. But what if you're a writer? If you're a writer with a talent for acting, it can be tough fending off all the flattering offers from a bunch of ambitious numbskulls. But acting doesn't have anything to do with intelligence. Most actors are extremely charming people. They don't even have to think; charm pours out of them, uncontrollably, like a disease. I'm a bit like that, or I can be, when I'm not scaring obnoxious women and their elderly-looking children at the post office.

Being a writer wouldn't stop wily theater types from trying to take advantage of Daphne's charm. The director of her *Measure for Measure* was obviously a classic creep; I got his number right away.

I used to go to theater in New York with my kids now and then, mostly because I thought it was good for them. I took my son to see *Fiddler on the Roof*. But the whole thing was a bit much for me. I'm half Jewish, but talk about taking advantage of Jewishness — it all becomes kind of anti-Jewish after a while. That is, when you figure out all the money they're making from doing the Hava Nagilah for the goyim. I don't know anyone who is really *that* Jewish actually. And so quaint about it too. My kid absolutely loved it though. A little too much. I was worried he might end up being enamored of the acting profession, like I was for a while.

Anyway, Daphne's director had them doing exercises — every bad director does. That was the thing that put me right off acting, having to get together in a group and swing your arms around, or improvising being at a party and saying corny things. He spent a whole day having them pick pieces of paper out of hat with only three words on them. Just "yes," "no," or "maybe." Then, each actor would have to go up on stage and say the word "yes," or "no," or "maybe" in one hundred different ways. A *hundred* times. The loser even invited Daphne up to his room once because he wanted to work on the "sexual energy" of her character. She wasn't naive; she went along with it because she thought it would be funny. It was. Apparently the guy made her sit on the couch and then he played a bunch of Frank Zappa records. "This," he said, "is real sex." He was such a loser that she used to joke about him in her letters. Still, I didn't trust him; I know how vulnerable kids like Daphne can be. I'm not so sure if she would have been quite as hip to his manipulations if it wasn't for me. But then again, you never know. She was a smart kid. I told her exactly what kind of guy he was. "Is he short, or skinny, or in some other way not quite physically up to par?" She said he was short and skinny. "Does he have wispy facial hair?" I asked. Sure enough he did. I told her to quit the play. She went on and did the performance. Of course, it was a horrible experience. But I respected her for making up her own mind; young people have to find these things out for themselves.

We thought exactly the same way about TV. The first time I talked to her on the phone I was completely charmed by her voice. It was small and quirky the way I expected it to be. At the time, *I Love Lucy* happened to be on — I used to watch reruns in the late afternoon. I told her it was the "Gobloots" episode. I didn't have to explain it. As soon as I said Gobloots, she knew what I meant. In it, Lucy is trying to put one over on Ricky, as usual, so she pretends that she's a kleptomaniac. The episode is fabulous, she wears thousands of costumes. At one point, she does a Tallulah Bankhead imitation, later she's riding around on a tricycle acting like a kid talking about how she was on the bus, and she saw a sign that said "Take one."

"So, I took one!" she says.

This was the beginning of her life of crime. And then at the end of the episode, Ricky decides to put one over on her. He puts a green lightbulb in the bedroom, and her skin looks green. Then he gets a fake doctor to tell her that she has the "Gobloots," that she caught from "the Booshoo Bird." It's priceless when Lucy says, "I got the Gobloots from the Booshoo Bird?" Daphne knew the episode by heart and recited all my favorite moments. I couldn't help testing her on other shows. She always passed. Like when we were talking about *The Andy Griffith Show* and I asked her if she remembered the time when Andy asked Opie to sit down and think about all the responsibilities of life. What did Opie say, after he'd thought for a minute? Daphne knew: "It kind of makes me sad, pa."

These are key, watershed moments. I know you're thinking: we liked the same sitcoms, so what? But there are good sitcoms and bad sitcoms. Most are bad. Even in the good ones there are only a few classic moments. If you have the taste and discretion to "get" things like this, then you've "got" me. When this happened, it was like *I* was the virgin, I wanted to open up to her like a flower. Never had I met anyone like this before, never. Chloe looked like the most perfect girl in the world — with the perfect sense of humor — but she proved to not be so perfect for me. This time, I was going about it in the right way. I was acquainting myself with Daphne's brain, with her interests, with her literary and intellectual passions first, then I would meet her in the flesh. It was her mind that I became obsessed with. I began inside and worked my way out. That's the way it should be. The body is only a convenient, sometimes incredibly inconvenient, casing for a possibly perfect soul. The outside doesn't matter; it doesn't have to match the inside. You can say I'm crazy to want to fall in love with someone who was my carbon copy. You can say that no two people are the same, people are different. But is it neurotic to search for a spiritual twin?

She wasn't a carbon copy anyway. She was eighteen years old when I met her. I was around fifty. I was male, she wasn't. So yeah, we were different. I didn't want her to be exactly like me, but Jesus, when you're walking around most of the time thinking that you're crazy because you love sitcoms, and old movies, and you hate people, and you can see through everyone, and you're so goddamn sensitive it's almost physically painful, and you just feel the constant need to express yourself on paper because it's the only place you actually feel alive — well, if you find a person who is going through exactly the same thing, can't you be forgiven for going a little nuts and wanting to hold them real close, so they never go away? She made me feel, for a moment, that maybe I had a place in the world. We were two people who just happened to find each other — although because of our strangeness, we were probably meant to spend our lives alone.

While nothing could have prepared me for Daphne's article, I was knocked out of my socks when I first met her. You could say she planned the whole thing, to seduce me, but I don't think of women like that. Men see them as evil temptresses half the time. That's just an excuse. Women can't help it if they're hypnotizing and gorgeous, can they? Especially when they are practically little girls. And, no matter what happened between Daphne and me later, there is no way I would ever accuse her of guile.

The dress was not like the one that Chloe wore when I first met her; in fact it was completely the opposite. It was a little girl's dress. Gingham, or organdy, or something, with ruffled sleeves. And it was cut in an "A" shape. It didn't look like she had any chest at all. She almost didn't, but what she had was hidden by the style of the thing. And printed on it were giant letters — the alphabet. It was like something you would see on *Sesame Street*. So she got me on two fronts with that dress — there was the innocence thing, and then the fact that she actually looked like a piece of writing. There were *letters* all over her. The choice of that dress was *some kind* of genius.

The effect was unfortunate in some ways. She came for the weekend. It's pretty amazing that her mother drove her up to stay with me for the weekend, but there you go. We spent a lot of time watching old movies. I introduced her to *The 39 Steps*, which she loved, and we had some ice cream from the local store. This is a complete no-no. I can't tell you how indigestible ice cream is. I taught her how to throw up by putting her finger down her throat. I know that sounds like an odd way to bond, but she was happy with the advice. She blamed me for it later. Then, of course, one thing led to another. I think it was the ABCs.

So here I was, within twenty-four hours into meeting her, eating ice cream, and gripped by an overwhelming sexual urge. I am completely aware of how hypocritical I must seem, even though I rail on and on about hypocrisy. Okay. I thought I wanted to meet her because my feelings for her were pure, and the first weekend I ended up in bed with her. Looking back, I suppose you could say I was fooling myself about my loneliness, and my pure motives. But I want you to look at the facts for a minute.

Even though I'll admit I desired her, we didn't have sex that night. She was incapable of having sex because she had a condition. We came to understand later that her vaginal muscles were much too tight for penetration. We never found out why. Anyway, the experiment we had that first weekend was the first and last time we came anywhere close to it. And yet I stayed with her for over a year. Now, doesn't that mean I had some kind of dedication to her?

I'll admit that at first I went a little crazy trying to cure her of her affliction. The next weekend she came down, I immediately tried to develop a homeopathic remedy, a simillimum. In order to do so, I had to figure out what kind of energy she had, whether or not she was a hot or cold person. I suspected she was cold, like me. Sometimes the questioning was pretty intense. Sometimes my questions felt like another way of making love, because I knew, somehow, that we were never going to have physical intercourse. If I was sitting with you, and I was at all interested in you, I'd question you too. Questioning is a way for me to get closer to people. I have an enormous amount of distrust, and seeing the blithe, unblinking way that Daphne gazed back at me when I asked her questions made me love her more.

Do you ever itch when you are coughing?

Do you find yourself waking up at night craving chocolate?

Does the smell of lavender make you sad?

Do crinkles on the sides of people's eyes frighten you?

Do you have cuticles?

Do you enjoy cutting bread at sunset?

What part of a flower attracts you the most?

Do you find the smell of the sea to be an aphrodisiac?

Do kitchen pans make you wheeze?

Does full-frontal nudity give you an urge to whine?

Do stained underpants cause your buttocks to break out?

What about bees — do you run, or stand still, or wave your arms and yell at them to go away?

Does dirt wash right off your skin?

Do you find yourself drawn to arachnids?

Are you afraid of grass?

How do you feel about green, in general?

Does mohair seem like an interruption, somehow?

Collecting things — an admirable hobby, or cause for concern?

Are you ever incontinent?

Do you ever flush before you finish peeing?

Do nights seem long?

Is the moon important, or inconsequential?

If I had a limp, would you laugh?

Do you ever scream at the sun?

The list went on and on. Some of the questions were even more personal, and difficult to answer. But Daphne endured. She seemed as eager as I was to cure herself. I was patient. But I wasn't completely stupid; a part of me also realized that God was showing me the way of all Zen. Why did I have to be so goal oriented? Could I manage to be in love with a girl *and* sexually attracted to her, but never have sex? I tried several simillimums on Daphne, but none worked. Finally, I put the questions away and settled into a sexless life with her. This means I was able to focus more on her development as a person.

That first summer she was working for the *New York Times* — they had commissioned several articles. The *Times* had also gotten her an apartment in the city, in return for some dog-sitting. I came down to visit her, and I even picked her up once or twice at the paper. No one knew who I was. My plan was working — it had been so long since I had had my picture taken, people no longer knew what I looked like. When someone asked who I was, I told Daphne to tell them my name was Alexander Fiddlehead. It was a pretty unlikely name, but it put people off the track and expressed my state of mind.

I have to say that from the beginning I had reservations about her working there. I thought she was wasting herself on the *Times*. It's not just that they've given me awful reviews, it's journalism in general. Of all the editors in the world, newspaper editors are the worst. It must be because of journalism schools. It reminds me of an incident with a magazine editor years ago. I wrote a short story about the war for the *Saturday Evening Post*. It wasn't all that good. Now, keep in mind, this was a *short story*. And not only was he crazy about deadlines, saying, "Get it in to me tomorrow, if not sooner," but then he wouldn't look at it for weeks and pointedly refused to call. Worse, when he finally did get back to me, he actually started talking about grabbing a hold of my audience in the first paragraph.

"You've got to grab them. You need a catchy lead!"

The whole idea of a "catchy lead" is one of the things I hate most about the modern world. Why not have a boring lead, or no lead at all, so that you can find out who the true, dedicated readers are?

Then he started on about fact checking.

"Is this the number of days you're allowed leave?"

"Yes," I said.

"How do you know?"

"I went to officer training school."

That wasn't good enough for him. "Do you have any documentation?"

Finally, he said he wanted me to fly my story by an Army instructor, just to confirm the details. I told him I thought he was nuts.

"We don't want to get sued," he said. This was the height of ridiculousness. Why would he get sued? It was a piece of fiction.

"The military can get touchy," he said. "It has to be authentic."

The devil isn't in the details, but stupid people sure are interested in them. I am, in my own way, a perfectionist — I worry about commas — but that doesn't stop me from realizing that a story can have all the commas in the right place, but still be a piece of garbage because it doesn't have anything to say. I distrust the whole idea of authenticity, actually — I think it's very inauthentic.

Sure, some clod has to be an investigative reporter. I just didn't think Daphne's brain was small enough. She was underselling herself. But we had some great times. I got a hotel room and stayed over one night so I could see her two days in a row. I told her that hotel rooms were places to commit suicide. She was alarmed when I said my room was on the twentieth floor. I even mentioned my fantasy about being in an Edward Hopper painting. You know, Daphne was the first person to make me think a hotel room could be a romantic place. She showed me her dolphin face. I was telling her how much I liked her picture on the magazine cover again — I used to tell her all the time — and how I fell in love with it. Then she did the face. Just like that.

She said, "You mean like this?" And there it was.

At first I was upset. "How can you do that on cue?" I asked.

She told me it was her "dolphin face." She explained that dolphins smile all the time even when they're in an enormous amount of pain, in captivity. The reason they always look like they're smiling is because their mouths stretch all the way across the sides of their heads. She explained that people always found her bright, and sweet, and pretty on the outside, even though she had a lot of pain inside. She used her rueful, dolphin face to convince people that she was uncomplicated and happy. I explained to her that I recognized right off that she was hiding a lot of pain. Sure, I was disconcerted that the face that I fell in love with was one she produced on cue, but it made a deadly hotel room charming for a minute or two.

There was also the night we met Doris. We were having a drink at one of those underground bars in Greenwich Village — it could have been my old apartment, actually — when this old lady walked in. She was probably only ten years older than I was. She had white hair cut in a bob and bangs, which was interesting in itself: it made her look like a dumpy old Coco Chanel. She sat down beside us, ordered a drink, and immediately tried to get us talking.

"I won't keep you for long," she said, "I know you're on a date."

I suppose we were. People who say they're not going to keep you for long are always pretty heartbreaking. You know they really want to keep you for ages; in fact, they want to move in with you and buy a dog.

Then she said, "I never come into Manhattan. I live in Queens, but I won on this card at the bingo." She took out a shiny little card with holes punched in it. "You can only get it redeemed on this here island, so I come in to get my money. That's all I wanted to tell you. It's good news. You can go back to your date now."

Naturally, it was sort of hard to go back to our date, because her presence was pretty overwhelming. She didn't stay long. She finished her drink, and waved goodbye to the bartender, and was on her way. Afterwards, the bartender took us into his confidence.

"Boy, you were lucky," he said.

"Why?"

"Lucky she didn't hit you over the head with her purse."

"Why would she do that?" I said.

"She's crazy," he said. "She had a lobotomy, years ago, when they were doing them, you know, to *that kind* of woman. Outspoken, like her. Didn't work, though. That's Doris. She was lying about never coming to Manhattan. She's been kicked out of every bar in town at one time or another, and she's barred from all of them."

I asked him why he let her in. "This bar just opened. She hasn't been kicked out of this one yet."

The encounter sparked an intense discussion. Daphne wanted to write a story about it, a political piece, all about women and feminism, and how women were kept down, and everything.

The idea nauseated me. "Why waste it," I asked, "and turn it into a human interest story? That would be very *authentic*."

"What's wrong with being authentic?" she asked.

"If you put it in a fictional story, let's say, buried in the middle of a novel, people would read it, and they wouldn't know it was real. You could change it any way you wanted, because you wouldn't have to be *authentic*."

"But why would you want to change it?" she asked.

"Because you could make it better. It would be less *authentic*, but more *sincere*. You could express its deeper meaning by lying."

It was an important lesson. And I knew she understood. It was also the first step in my project to woo her away from the world of journalism.

⸺

In case you were wondering, that story is true. But also, it's not. That is, when I wrote, I added something. But the added stuff only serves to make it truer. It's not *authentic*, but it is *sincere*. And no, it's not the lobotomy part.

⸺

137

The next thing you know, Daphne got an offer to write a story about the Democratic Convention in Miami. *Ms. Magazine* wanted her to be their *youth* reporter. I told her not to do it, that it would take her away from what she was hoping would be a larger project, a book about her life so far.

I thought her book could be great, truly great. As you can see, I was trying to gently push her away from nonfiction altogether. It wasn't just that journalism was full of never-wases. It's that it was only in fiction she could speak the truth. So how could she speak honestly in a memoir? It seemed to me that she could turn it into fiction. The truth about my novels is that they are about my life. Maybe not the details, but certainly my emotional reality.

This book, for example, contains the truth about my emotional life, but not everything in it is true. Things have been altered to make them more sincere and less authentic, but I don't want that to send you on a quest to figure out what's not true or what is.

At this point she did the first thing that really made me doubt her. I saw it as a minor mistake — after all, she was young, and easily seduced by the world. Later incidents made me realize the true significance of this early act. When she was deciding whether to write the article about the Miami convention, she was staying at my place on weekends. So she called me from Manhattan during the week and asked me if she could give my phone number to her agent, so he could contact her on the weekend. Agents? Worse than editors, the scum of the earth.

"What do you need an agent for?" I asked.

"Someone has to handle my contracts."

"You should do that," I said. "Or I'll help you. You don't want an agent. Some slimy bastard who wants to make money off you."

I was irritated, but I calmed down. I told myself she didn't understand how evil those people were, or the pain any unnecessary contact with them caused me. I told her under no circumstances could she give my number to the slop bucket. No, no, no!

She went off to Miami for a week, and we continued to write letters and talk on the phone. I think she was learning a lot. She insisted that she could write the truth in non-fiction, and that it offered her tremendous opportunity for detail and observation. *I* made the observation that the temptation in her nonfiction was to be clever. It's a huge problem, even for the best writers. The best writers are all about style — their work is style-obsessed, baroque. I, for instance, cannot pick up a book if it doesn't have a specific rhythm and tone. Writers must have their own trademarks; writers must have an ear for sound. You could tell any book written by Virginia Woolf for instance, its gentle nuances. Evelyn Waugh has his lilting, dry sarcasm. Hemingway the famous, lean, parched sentences. So, if you're a writer, you want to find your own rhythm. The problem is that you become hypnotized by that style and become cute. There is also the danger of cuteness of content. There's something funny — an observation let's say — that becomes a great joke. You can't resist it. But both in the case of style, and in the case of humor, the key question is, does it serve the whole? Is it cute for cuteness' sake, or is it for the sake of truth? I told her that she had written one entertaining little piece about her youth, but that it was, unfortunately — though entertaining, and delightful, and quirky in its own way — still ultimately superficial.

Her mother too, called herself a writer. She had written a truly horrible book about raising her own children. It was completely self-serving and trite. Daphne loved her mother's book. I couldn't tell her outright that it was a piece of crap, but instead tried gently to nudge her into discovering it for herself. Her father was an former art teacher who ended up chasing young women. He was also prone to drinking, and going into rages. It's pretty amazing that Chloe and Daphne had similar parents: creative, imperfect, worldly people, encouraging their precocious girls to be artists — ultimately to serve their own egos. God help me if my children ever decide to write. I wouldn't wish it on either of them. I have my own agonizing life, why would I want it for them? Any parent who actually wishes their child was a writer, actor, or artist of any kind is nuts — worse, they're pathological, living through the kid in the worst way. Most people think art equals fame. Really, it equals torture.

Anyway, here was Daphne with this dark and daffy family, and all she really got in her little autobiographical piece was the daffy part. She did that admirably, and she probably she didn't want to hurt them. But artists can't worry about hurting people. That's why they lie — so they can tell the truth. Ultimately, it means that writing must not be about serving your own ego. It can't be about making pretty things; it has to be about pulling back the Band-Aid so that people can see the sore.

I think she got all this in Miami, and she began to be turned off by the falseness of the political situation, how ultimately hopeless it all was. And then there was the whole idea of her being a "youth reporter." She should have been a *reporter*. That's journalism for you — let's get the youth angle, the black angle, the woman's angle. Don't they understand that as long as these things are just "angles," they're completely useless? I think she felt bad about taking on the job in the first place. I told her not to worry about it. What was done was done, and she had an obligation after all. I told her to forgive herself; we all have to forgive ourselves from time to time. She had the same problem I do; that's what made it so damned difficult and touching at the same time. Christ, but the whole thing made me want to cry. I realized that she and I were exactly the same. We want to please people. We're nice; we want other people to be happy. The contradiction is that our work is mainly about the imperfections of the world, how horrible it is. So cuteness, in our writing, is always a temptation. Not that there can't be any cuteness, but we have to curtail it because sometimes we just want to be loved. And a good writer is never loved.

Feared, yes; hated, yes; but never unconditionally loved.

The result? I desperately wanted Daphne to move in with me. It was obvious that the world was pulling her in so many ways, and that the only way I could protect her from all that temptation would be if she was away from it. In the fall, she was supposed to go back to Yale. Soon the summer would be over, and she would be gone. God, I can't tell you what it was like driving her back to college. She had stayed in my house almost continuously after the convention, and I couldn't imagine her going back. When we arrived at her dormitory I wanted to kick every Joe College Type in the neck. They all looked self-satisfied and happy. All those potential Section Men.

Fortunately, Daphne realized that her book was more important than Yale, and she only stayed there a month before she finally agreed to move in with me.

———

As excited as I was to be living with another writer, the book we were focused on also became the flashpoint for some fundamental differences. It's difficult for me to write about it now — it's all relatively recent. In the first month we were living together, she did a horrible thing. Why do we put up with it when lovers do horrible things? Looking back on it we say, "I should have known. I should have taken it as a sign." Why is it that we forgive them? Because we're lonely and desperate. And the lesson that has to be learned is that no person is really perfect, and even if they seem perfect, there will always be something. But I was deluded. Anyway, things were going well at first, and then — unbelievable, shockingly — her editor called her and asked her if, since I were living with her and all, it might be possible for me to write a blurb for her book.

A blurb.

God, how I hate that word. Think about it, about what a "blurb" really is. Sounds harmless, doesn't it? It's a money person, some goddamned accountant, asking a creative person if they will read someone else's book and supply them, you know, with a little statement that summarizes how wonderful that book is. You know what blurbs are really all about, don't you? Pick up a book and turn it over and encounter things like: "Pressed into this picaresque romp is all the excitement of juvenile discovery, all the joy of learning, growing, and realizing. Yes, the wise-beyond-her-years Daphne Willickers has come up with a gem." That's what I could have written — if I was an idiot.

How are you supposed to summarize a novel and its effect on you in one paragraph? Half the time, writers don't even read the novels they're sent to write blurbs for. But that doesn't stop them from writing that garbage. If you're asked to write a blurb you're supposed to like the novel. If you don't, you're not supposed to write anything. But that's not what happens. Writers — as a favor to their fellows — will write a positive blurb about any piece of trash if it serves their careers. But the killer, the canker in this casual suggestion, was how it suddenly reduced our relationship to commerce, to the cold reality of a monetary exchange. I'd sooner have my heart ripped out, and laid all fresh and bleeding on a table.

I cannot tell you how deeply offended I was. Actually, it wasn't the suggestion, it was the fact that Daphne asked me. How could I not question her motives? I'd only known her for nine months, and for three of those we'd merely exchanged phone calls and letters. Have you ever experienced the nagging, aching feeling that you're devoting your life to someone who is using you? Such a thing wouldn't be possible if the world wasn't an evil place, if behind all social interactions there wasn't the possibility of advantage, greed, and ambition. I blame the world. The idea that Daphne could or ever would possibly use me was too horrible to imagine, so I put it out of my mind. But it lurked, always. You know, it was one thing for Chloe to have the modeling business tugging at her. I didn't understand that world. I knew it was awful, but it's hard to completely hate the unfamiliar. I was familiar — far too familiar, let me tell you — with the world of agents, and publishers, and editors. I had fought all my life to keep them at a distance and not let them contaminate my writing. And yet there was Daphne, practically inviting them over for dinner.

What kept us going for a while was the idea of having a baby. I know, like every other thing I say, it sounds crazy. But we both believed in it for a while. It was something separate from the world of writing. I couldn't even have sex with her, how could we ever produce a child? I suppose that could have been what it was really about — solving the sex problem. Daphne told me that she was having dreams about us having a baby. Sure, I already had two children. They were both in their teens, and certainly more than enough for me to deal with. But a baby with Daphne came to symbolize something that we could do, positively, together, when the difficulties with her writing became insurmountable.

Like getting into a huge argument about French criticism. She was reading something by Roland Barthes. God, that stuff is evil. She started talking about the supremacy of style over content. The kind of pretentious crap I hate, the idea that a perfect sentence is paramount. The truth is, it's not. And yet it is. That is, something can sound wonderful, but who cares if it's got nothing to say? These French critics go on and on about the death of meaning. Oh yeah, great. Great for you, living in your ivory tower, but how do you plan to live your life without meaning? Section Men of the worst kind. I knew Daphne knew what I was saying about those French idiots, but she was reluctant to give it up. Why? Because these ideas sounded pretty. That says it, completely. *They sound pretty, but they're not ideas at all.*

So how does all this relate to the baby? Well, when we'd get into these arguments about style and content, it was becoming increasingly clear to both of us — even though we wouldn't say it — that she was hypnotized by this bilge and I was violently opposed to it. I threw a goddamn lamp once, I really did. When she started to quote Roland Barthes, I picked up a lamp, and threw it at the wall, and it shattered into a thousand pieces. I said, "No, no, you don't need meaning . . . no. What do you need with meaning?" And there we were, sitting in the dark.

When we talked about the baby, things weren't violent. She had a dream and the baby was called Seraphim. I don't know why we would have a Spanish baby, but it was so far removed from our reality at that point that it seemed right. We not only had a name for it, but we talked about how she — it would have to be a she — would grow up and not be an artist. The last thing we would want would be for her to write. We talked about how she would live on nuts and berries and walk around in bare feet — I could never get Chloe to allow me to let my children go all natural, they still craved burgers and fries. We figured at one point the kid would want to go off and live in a tent in the woods. And we would let her.

But I think the fact that she was imaginary was what we both liked best, deep down. It became sad and painful, but we couldn't stop talking about it. We loved that little girl who didn't exist more than we loved anything else in this horrible world — but not more than we loved our love, which, ultimately, I guess, didn't exist anymore.

There, I said it.

Each time you fall out of love, it chips away at your confidence in your ability to connect. It's all fine and good for people to say that you can go through therapy to get over it. But no matter what you say, *it's a failure*, and in my case it was a failure at something that I don't have much confidence in anyway. I'm ashamed to say that I became pretty desperate after the first year or so with Daphne, because inside I knew it was crumbling.

The angst centered on the phone. The damn phone.

Phones are evil things, and I shouldn't even have had one. Chloe insisted that if the children were staying with me I had to have one in case there was an emergency.

"A small price to pay," she said.

Right. But it was a huge price, because that little black thing drove a wedge between Daphne and me. And that finally drove us apart.

Soon, Daphne's book was in galleys. This meant that all the final changes were being made. I can't say I really liked her book — which is an amazing thing for me to admit, but honest. At the time, I told myself it was the best she could do. Looking back, I realize that wasn't true. There was some real charm in it, until her editor got at it. He tried to get her to use longer words. I had spent a lot of time telling her the simplest word would do. But she wanted to get the damn thing published, and you don't get published, and you don't get respect unless you use long words — unless you're *literary*.

Because that's what writing's all about isn't it? Pull out your thesaurus. Thank you, Roget.

Anyway, it was almost a year into our relationship when her editor called her and told her they wanted to interview her on the radio all about "the sixties." I was there when she got the call; I witnessed the whole thing. I know about Daphne's little dolphin face, so she couldn't pull any tricks on me. I could tell she was damned excited. Thrilled actually. Thrilled to her little dolphin blowhole about a goddamn radio interview. And she resented me. I could tell. She resented that I wasn't happy for her. What did she think I was, jealous? Really, I think if I ever had to go through another interview, it would kill me.

It was a rude awakening, an act of pure ego. And it was no good forgiving her. It's not as if she hadn't been warned by me, a thousand times. About how these horrible things ruin your life and your work.

Still, I conceived the Florida plan.

I got it in my head — this was how gone I was — that if we had a baby it would solve everything. The baby became more real than our relationship, and I had no idea what I was doing. Naturally, in order to get a baby, we would have to have actual intercourse. Maybe I was just being driven crazy by having such a tempting girl around all the time, sleeping with her, for Christ's sake, but never really doing anything. For whatever insane reason, I discovered a homeopathic doctor in Florida. A neighbor recommended him, a midwife who was quite knowledgeable — and I thought if we went to Florida, maybe Daphne could get treatment, and maybe we could have intercourse. At the very least we would get away from the house for a while. That's how bad it was. The precious house that I loved so much — I wanted to get away from it.

Anyway, my kids had wanted to go to Florida. My daughter wanted to check on some universities, and my son was still at an age when a vacation in Florida was the height of adventure. So I figured I could kill lots of birds with one stone. I'd take my kids on a vacation — which would be bearable because Daphne was along. And Daphne and I would be in Florida together to deal with the baby thing — which would be bearable because the kids were there.

When I look back now, it all seems demented, but you don't know these things at the time.

Before we left there was one more phone incident. This time I picked up. It was someone from the *New York Times*. The *New York Times* talking to me *at my house*. Of course, they were calling for Daphne. I handed the phone over to her, but when she hung up, I raised the roof. I tried to explain to her the importance of what had happened. The *New York Times* had spoken to me at my house! I think she thought I was overreacting.

We got to Florida and everything was fine. Don't worry, I was decent about sleeping arrangements — I'm not an idiot. I slept with my son, and my daughter slept with Daphne. I wasn't going to be in the same bed with her on vacation and have them imagine what was going on. I don't think my daughter was pleased. She and Daphne didn't have much in common, even though they were essentially the same age.

We ambled along, and did the swimming thing, which we all enjoyed. Growing up, I spent summers at the beach, and I still find it calming. It's like the woods — if it wasn't for the damn people. The turning point revolved around two things. The trip to the acupuncturist, and *The Heartbreak Kid*.

After we went swimming, Daphne often went to the homeopathic doctor. I always accompanied her. I felt it was as much my problem as hers, and besides I didn't want the doctor to get up to any hanky-panky. I would wait patiently while Daphne got her treatment. The doctor decided on acupuncture, which was a pretty revolutionary remedy at the time in America, but it made a lot of sense to me. After we'd gone there for about five sessions, it happened. The receptionist came up to me and whispered, "Excuse me."

I said, "Yes?"

"The young lady would like to speak to you sir."

"Why?"

"She said that it was 'urgent.'"

I said, "Isn't she getting acupuncture right now?"

And she said, "Yes, but, well . . . I think it's important that you speak to her."

Fine. So I got up and went into the little doctor's office and there was Daphne lying on the table. Now, I knew a little bit about acupuncture but I wasn't prepared for what I saw. I knew that the doctor starts out with only one or two pins in one or two places, and then as the days go by, increases the number of pins and the depth of application. When I opened the door, the doctor was standing with his back to me, preparing some pins. Daphne was lying on the table on her back. She was decent, thank God; the doctor had contrived to keep her dignity intact with pretty artful placing of a towel. But it looked to me like every part of her body that was exposed was covered with pins. And I could see that the pins were in there pretty deep. And she was crying. The tears were streaming down her face. She said my name, and I responded to it, and then she said my name again and, "It hurts." And I said I know it hurts honey, but we agreed we were going to try everything. And she said, "No, I can't, I can't do this. I just can't." And she cried some more. Jesus, what was I supposed to do? An eighteen-year-old girl laid out practically naked on a table weeping and saying, "I can't do this." No, I don't have a heart of stone, and I couldn't go on. I thanked the good doctor, told him we were finished; he took the pins out, and we left.

That was it. Our last attempt.

We walked back to the hotel in silence. How could we lie to each other?

How could the baby be a comforting fantasy now? We'd tried everything. A few months earlier, I might have said, "Don't worry, honey, we'll try something else." But Florida was it, and we both knew it. If either of us ever mentioned the baby again, we would both have broken down. You can go through anything with someone if you think they're a kindred spirit. But months earlier I'd given up the idea that we were true landsmen. I had met her when she was too young, that was the problem. At least that's what I told myself. These days, I'm not even sure if Daphne was really a good person. That's how bad it is.

If the acupuncture was sad, *The Heartbreak Kid* was worse. When we got back to the hotel room, the kids had ordered a pizza — that was bad, it's like pouring acid into your stomach — because they wanted to go out to see *The Heartbreak Kid*, a movie directed by Elaine May. I'd always been a fan of

Elaine May, but I was suspicious of the title. I was feeling a little bit too heartbroken myself.

I can't tell you how painful it was. It wasn't that the movie was wonderful. But it was so *appropriate*. What happened in the movie was exactly what was happening to us. The similarity was perfectly clear, to me at least. I don't know if it was clear to Daphne because she sure was pretty surprised by what happened afterwards.

In the movie this guy — Charles Grodin is great, he underplays everything — is on his honeymoon with his wife, played by Jeannie Berlin. Berlin is the classic annoying girl, and you have to wonder why the guy married her. Grodin is perfect for the leading man because he always seems so put upon and reasonable. Anyway, the first day of their honeymoon, his young wife lies out in the sun too long and gets a terrible burn. It's a classic honeymoon mishap — you can't touch anybody with such terrible sunburn and, on top of that, Jeannie Berlin smears herself all over with Noxzema. She looks like she just walked out of *Night of the Living Dead*. It was very funny. Then, who does Charles Grodin meet but Cybill Shepherd? She's the only disappointing part of the movie. She reminds me of a Roland Barthes sentence: beautiful but empty.

There were so many similarities.

I couldn't touch Daphne ever again, the trip to the doctor had made that clear, and the truth was, I had fallen out of love. The world had worn me down; as far as I was concerned she might as well have been covered with Noxzema from head to toe. Have you ever had that experience — going to see a movie that so accurately reflects your mood that you feel like you haven't been at a movie at all, but burrowed more intensely into your own conflicts?

I felt more trapped than Charles Grodin. Everything was falling apart, I couldn't be myself anymore — Daphne was making me feel that it was unreasonable of me to rant and rail against her agent, her editor, and the *New York Times*. Her book was going to end up like her mother's — the worst type of memoir, filled to the brim with cuteness and lies. I couldn't stand it any longer. But always, always, even at moments like this, what keeps hitting you in the face is the potential. It was there when we first met: the little girl standing in my house in the alphabet dress. But I had to remember that potential was not reality, and that the girl that I was in love with in my head was not Daphne.

I told her to leave.

"Go back to my house," I said, refusing to use the word home, "and clear out." I didn't say, "And never come back." I wanted to, but I knew that would be too cruel.

She asked why. As if she didn't know.

I didn't know what to say, so I said that I couldn't have any more children. I tried to give her the idea that my own children were driving me crazy because they wanted to go to the movie and order pizza. "I'm through with children," I said. "I'm too old. I can't go through it again." I tried to put it on myself, which I felt was pretty big of me. But you know, when you're going through a breakup like that you're just sleepwalking anyway, nobody is in their right mind. It's so horrible to imagine that what's happening is really happening, that the nightmare has become a reality, that all you can do is hope you don't bump into each other or fall down and hurt yourself. You're simply numb with pain and grief.

When I got back, she was gone. I heard from her several times afterwards. She called to ask for advice about her book — the last thing I wanted to talk to her about. I tried to be nice, even though I was furious. I turned on the charm. This was a bad thing, because she started to call me more often and suggested that we be friends. She even got a house of her own in the country, not that far from where I lived. It was insane. As if she really wanted to be by herself — she was always waiting by the phone at my place for that call from New York. She came to visit me once. It was terrible. Thankfully my daughter was there and I pretended we had to leave, so the meeting ended quickly. After that, I was brusque with her on the phone, there was no other way to get rid of her. I have a trick with people like that, and it's something I had told Daphne about. When someone is really irritating me, I say to them, "Listen, don't bother calling me back. Why don't I call you?" Daphne knew that I never call anyone.

"Okay," she said cheerily. I'm sure it wasn't until she hung up that she realized she'd never hear from me again.

I've pretty much said it all now. There doesn't seem to be much reason to go on. But I guess I should tell you about Pegeen.

For a few years, I was devastated. There was no hope. It seemed to me that there was nothing left except work. I kept telling myself that writing should be enough, but then I would go crazy with loneliness. Hey, look at me, a hopeless romantic who hates people. You've got to wonder how God gets the ideas in his head for these fantastically complicated jokes. He must laugh like hell. It should be obvious that I'm not cut out for a certain type of love, there's no "Mrs. Right" for me. The nice way to explain it would be that my standards are too high. But that's something I will never admit. I simply can't stop dreaming about what might be.

So I did what many people do; I settled. Daphne was my last attempt; I was too old to make a fool of myself over my imagined, perfect love.

Anyway, like I said, it was a few years later. I was riding the bus back to town. I met a girl. She was nice. Pegeen. It didn't take me too long to figure out that there was nothing special about her except the fact that she was young and beautiful.

There was that.

At the time she was on her way to a fair in Dartmouth. We had a friendly, warm talk, not about anything in particular. God, I was lonely. I gave her my address and we exchanged letters.

She had been working as an au pair in Massachusetts, but she was on her way back to Baltimore, she was from there, where she'd married some guy. He was a pitiful character. At times I feel guilty for taking her away from him. But not for long. What could I do? He sounded nice enough. And I don't say that about many people, as you know. He had a child by another woman who deserted him, and he and Pegeen were going to raise the child together. He also had one kidney and was on dialysis. You might think I was cruel to woo her away from someone who had already been ditched once and only had one malfunctioning kidney. But what can I say? If you haven't figured it out, I'm handicapped in some very basic way. What I've got is as bad as missing a kidney. I've been ditched far too many times, if not by girls, then by love itself. I felt sorry for him. But like all human beings, I felt sorrier for myself.

I even thought about James Joyce and Nora Barnacle. She used to make fun of his novels. She was right, as far as I'm concerned. But the point is, she had no idea what he did. Pegeen makes quilts. She makes nice quilts. But it's my observation that people who excel at things like that are generally content, and can never know or understand what it means to be an artist.

I'm not worried that Pegeen will read this. I don't think she would be hurt. She seems happy to save me from my loneliness.

I've gone back and reread everything several times — you know, the commas — and I don't really know why I've written this.

I swore it was something I would never write.

And yet I had to.

Let me tell you, that's reason enough.

Is it good? I don't think that applies here. I don't expect anyone to ever read it anyway, and I really don't know if I want anyone to.

———

There is one thing.

I realize, looking back at this, that I've mentioned the war several times — held it out, and dangled it in front of you as if I was going to write about it. Well, I can't. Honestly, there's no point. I would like to say that there's something of the horror of war in this. That would be selling war short, though. Especially the one I was involved in. But there is some truth in a statement like that — in the sense that in all human relations there is the same brutality which characterizes the worst of combat.

It isn't a nice way to end, but there you have it.

———

I tried. I really tried to stop. I put this away for a while. But in the interim — what a lovely phrase, "in the interim," it covers so much, but not enough — several things have happened.

There have been books written about me.

I don't want to dignify them by mentioning them. I will tell you that they were the ultimate betrayal, but I'm not going to say that I came back to this because of them. That would be giving those books too much credit. And it's not true.

No, the reason I've returned is that this isn't over.

More than that, though, I started thinking about you.

Has a book ever been written in the second person? I'm

not sure. So much talk about the first and third person — but never the second — except for instruction manuals and religious tracts, I guess. It seems to me it's time someone tried. I read and reread all those things I said about not caring whether anybody read this, about my lack of concern for an audience. But if you read between the lines you'll see that though I don't give a crap about my audience, I do, in fact, care about you. It's not that I was lying. There are no lies in this; only untruths.

Reading what I've written, it's clear that I've written it for you, whoever you are. I'm not going to describe you — you don't need to be described to yourself. But as you've been reading this, you've known all along that it was written for you, and that you were meant to read it. You know that I've been reaching out to you across these pages, if for no other reason than to relieve my unbearable loneliness. I can't think of any other reason for writing really. At least for the moment of putting the words down on the page, you don't feel so alone. But I won't say that. I want to go one step further and say that the book is addressed to you, and you are real, and you are out there, and there is the possibility that we will meet.

There, I said it.

I just want to be honest.

This brings me to the war. The last ending was a prevarication. I was hedging. I think I knew that I had to write about the war, but not write about it at the same time — something I think you'll understand. In case you don't, I mean that by writing about the essence of what the war was for me, not the details, I might get to something.

I arrived at the war late, 1943. My writing was at the end of its adolescence. I had several stories published, and was beginning to make money. It was an exciting time for me. The thought of not going to war never crossed my mind. Don't imagine it was the cause — don't imagine it was about the Jews. I know that sounds like a terrible thing to say, but as a half-Jew, I take full responsibility for it. The war wasn't about the Jews for me. I was never all that fond of my father, and he was a Jew. I'm not saying that it was his Jewishness that I wasn't fond of. I'm saying that I had no familial affection for my religion, or any sense of belonging to a race. There was Hitler, he was evil. It was simply the right thing to do.

I don't mean to make myself sound heroic; I wasn't. I did what I had to do. In that way, the war was like writing. God, you don't want a medal for it. If you're waiting for medals, then you're the worst kind of scum, worse than the enemy. And please don't think I'm writing about the war because it's noble or a proper subject for literature. I admire Hemingway's style, but hey, I'm just not his kind of guy. I was never someone who enjoyed the brotherhood of violence and competition. I hate all that — so you can imagine what the war was like for me. I don't in any way mean to glamorize it. Like those John Wayne movies. Anyone who was really involved in the war will tell you that those movies are garbage. Please don't think that I'm writing about the war because I think it's important, or thrilling, or a great experience, or something I'm proud of. It isn't any of those things, and I'm not.

But you know that.

I applied to officer's training school. Not because I was a

coward, or privileged. Okay, I was privileged, or I wouldn't have been able to apply. But I wasn't a coward. Not that it would have mattered. I applied and was accepted, but I wasn't called up for a while. I wouldn't have been any use to anyone as a private. At that time we didn't have any idea about horrors like D-day, it wasn't on my mind to save myself from that. Anyway, I was there, and no one could have imagined it. I took a ten-week course in Georgia and became a flight instructor for a while. Then I went to Maryland to train as a special agent in counterintelligence.

I quickly discovered I was suited to the job, interrogating and processing prisoners of war and suspects.

Once we landed at Utah Beach and started making our way through France, I began my job. I don't mind saying I was good at it. I was too damn good. If you haven't figured it out already, I can be pretty ruthless; I've got someone's number about five minutes after I've met them. This isn't a really great talent to have in the real world — there doesn't seem to be much point in getting to know anyone when you can figure out their story in the first five minutes, even if it's almost always a pretty sad tale. But in counterintelligence, it's a gift. Back then, I was young, and handsome, and charming, and there was no way anyone knew when I was onto them. This is great if you want to wrestle secrets out of people. It's also ideal for a writer, because you get to hear their pitiful stories, and their self-justifications, all the other crap that makes people human, and then you peel it all away. The great thing is that you're not involved with the person at all — you don't love them or anything, you don't want them as a friend. So the very thing that used to drive me crazy all the time — the fact

that I could see into people's hearts and was generally disgusted, made me the perfect counterintelligence officer.

Again, I'm not bragging.

You know I'm not.

But like I said, I'm not going to go on and on about the
war. You can go to some other book for that. I'll just say that
it was more horrible than you can imagine. The casualties, as
we plowed through France and into Germany, were about
twenty-five percent. That's a lot of dying. The Battle of
Hurtgen Forest almost did me in, along with many other
decent, ordinary young guys. If it wasn't the trench foot, it
was the bleakness of it all. Everywhere you looked: death.

For me, the breaking point was Treblinka. I was one of the
first to walk into that place — not that I'm proud of it. I'm
not ashamed to admit that I couldn't take it. Have you ever
smelled burning flesh? You might think that hating people
like I do, the whole thing would have been a perverse treat. I
can almost understand why you might think that. But it's
important for you to hear, again: I don't hate mankind, just
people. I understand now what I went through and why I had
a breakdown — because that's what happened. It's because a
concentration camp was the logical extension of all my minor
irritations with publishers, and Section Men, and every other
idiot I've ever met. I think I realized that I had, once or twice
in my life, imagined doing this to people. How many times
had I wanted to kick in somebody's head or see them turning
on a spit?

Plenty.

And have you ever felt that way? I think so. It's in all of
us. Don't lie. That's why what happened after the war was so

stupid, all that demonizing of the Germans. There's nothing wrong with Germans. I like them. I liked them too damn much, as you'll see. *They're* the nation of shopkeepers. This isn't a contradiction at all. Yes, they've produced some of the greatest artists that have ever lived. I'm not real fond of Mozart, Beethoven, or Wagner — though Schubert is okay — but the reason these guys were so technically good at what they were doing is that they applied the dedication of shop-keepers, that insane concern over detail, to *art*. You have to admire that. Nothing gets by these people, their national economy will always be in great shape — when they're not an occupied country — because they're so damned hard-working and thorough. Most people are sloppy and silly. Not Germans. This is the reason why they had it in for the Jews. The Jews were better shopkeepers, and that pissed the Germans off. But to say that there is something in the German character that is essentially bad is stupid. "Oh no, it's not me, it's the Germans. We don't have to worry about a second Holocaust, because we're watching the Germans." Right. God, every time I read an article about young German skinheads, or anti-Jewish stuff in contemporary Germany, I get irate. Leave the Germans alone. Look at yourself. Christ, you can spend day and night watching the Germans, making sure they don't kill any more Jews, while you're off killing blacks or homosexuals or, even more likely, making a buck by ruining your best friend.

Sometimes I don't know why I bother to explain things like this to you. I think it's because I imagine you nodding your head and agreeing. And then I feel better.

Anyway, Treblinka did a tremendous number on me. I

couldn't sleep. I sure didn't buy any of that "Germans are demons" stuff. Not even Hitler.

Let's talk about him. I not implying Hitler was a great guy, but he was *human*. Not much different than most people. Failed painter, bitter, thought he'd make a grab for power any way he could — sound like anyone you know? Every guy you meet on the street, that's who.

The problem was, I couldn't do what most people did. I couldn't blame someone else. I blamed myself. And I'm not making myself out to be a saint here. It always has been my problem. I'm always examining myself, judging myself, trying to be a better person. Treblinka didn't teach me any-thing about Hitler or the Germans. But it taught me a lot about myself. And I didn't like what I saw.

So I ended up in an army hospital, to receive treatment for battle fatigue. I didn't want to be there, but I didn't have any choice. When you haven't slept for a week, the result is that you can't move or talk — you need a sedative. But after I'd recovered, I realized that they were dead set on giving me a psychiatric discharge. I didn't want that.

I know that looks like pride, but it wasn't. And I admit pride. I can take great pride in a sentence, or in the perfect description of a character; and that's bad, soul-destroying. Let me tell you, I'm more than aware of my tendency towards that kind of pride. But soldier pride, pride in service to your country, hell, I don't believe in that bunk. There's a job. It just wasn't fair that I'd been in the service for almost two years, been through hell and barely made it back, and then I was to go home in disgrace. It wasn't fair, and it wasn't accurate.

If you're looking for the origins of my pathological hatred

of the psychiatric profession, you'd probably find it right
there. I mean, there you are, in a bed, in Germany, feeling like
a piece of crap, worrying that they'll send you home as a nut-
case, and what do they do? Sic a bunch of hopeless psychiatrists on you. I'll never forget those guys. They were all
ugly as sin. Is that some sort of requirement for the job? I
always think of that great scene in *Miracle on 34th Street*
when they send the guy who thinks he's Santa Claus to a
shrink. That scene is perfect, and it encapsulates everything I
think about these muddle-headed creeps. If you'll remember,
the crazy Santa Guy, who isn't crazy at all, is cool as a cucum-
ber — stroking his beard — while the psychiatrist is an itchy
guy with a facial tic. Santa ends up psychoanalyzing the
doctor, of course. I'd say that psychiatrists are like the kids
you used to beat up in school. The thing is, they're the type
of guys who grow up and people still beat up on them. At
least I do.

Boy, did I put one over on them. One of the psychiatrists
had a stutter. I'm not kidding. I don't know much about stut-
ters, but doesn't that qualify as a mental illness? It's not a
physical problem is it? Don't stutterers usually have a dad
that bullied the hell out of them? Wow, what a perfect
person to help you with your problems! Just like Santa, I
ended up feeling sorry for him. But not for long. And the
second one was a disgusting sensualist. You could tell.
Sensualists are fleshy, they have big lips, and their skin is
oily. He was a pervert, that was evident, and he smelled. I
don't know if it was his breath or his clothes or what. All I
could think was, this guy is into something that's really disgusting and makes him smell. Or else he doesn't know

enough to wash. Inspires confidence, right? The third one was a sadist. Clearly. He sure looked like he would have been great SS material. He didn't talk much, but he had his little notepad, and he let the other guys play bad cop. All the while he was calling the shots, judging, and smiling.

They asked me all sorts of questions about my family, naturally. Was I ready for *them*? I poured on the charm and acted intelligent. They couldn't believe how self-possessed I was. And I didn't say a word against my family, because there's nothing wrong with them. My mother is the salt of the earth — you'd be lucky to have a mother like her, a perfect person, always loving, and caring, and worrying. And my sister, heart of gold, doilies and all. I've always loved her to death. It was a bit harder with my dad. But I don't hate him. He's a good man. I can say that without lying. I never lied to these guys. I'm not a good liar. My father is a good man — normal as hell, but good. I was always completely honest.

The wunderkinds didn't think to ask me how I felt about people in general though. It must be in the goddamn psychiatric manual that everybody's problems are related to their family. Not mine. Now if these geniuses had bothered to ask me how I felt about my fellow man, or how I felt about Treblinka, they would have got an earful. I don't think I would have been able to hide my feelings, even with all my tact. But that didn't matter anyway because they didn't ask me.

"Did you love your parents?"

"Sure, they're a couple of peaches, swaying on a tree!"

"Then you're healthy, soldier, go on back to work."

So I did.

I was very proud.

Our job after the war was mopping up. For counterintelligence, that meant we were supposed to arrest members of the Nazi party and question them. It's not as clear-cut as it sounds. Lots of people were members of the Nazi party. I know that might sound strange, but it's true. It's one thing to blame all Germans; it's another thing to blame the ones who were members of the party. Shouldn't *they* have known what was going on?

Okay, the shoes you're wearing were made by people who earn ten cents a day and consider themselves lucky. Every time you eat a hamburger, you're killing some defenseless cow that never hurt you. In order to get elected, politicians have to tax the poor like crazy, and give all sorts of benefits to the rich, because the rich vote, and the poor don't. We all sort of know these things, but do we do anything about it? No. Why? Because we're human, and that means we're selfish, and shortsighted, and ultimately couldn't care less about anything but our own skins. I'm always amazed at how the German people are supposed to be held to some sort of standard that we would never apply to ourselves.

There were Germans who were psychopaths, just like there are Americans who are psychopaths. There were Germans who were directly involved, and then there was the vast majority of Germans who were merely going about their daily lives, like you and me, who didn't want to rock the boat. Most members of the Nazi party fell into the last category, only a handful fell into the first two categories. It was my job to separate the wheat from the chaff.

I enjoyed it. I didn't work alone, naturally. There was always an interpreter. Mine was a nice, big, strapping guy. He had a minor visual impairment that meant he couldn't work on the front lines. I used to look at him and think: it's boys like him that usually die first. God, he was lucky. But he was a good interpreter; he did his job and kept quiet, so that I felt like there was nobody else in the room. He had to be good at his job, because even the slightest mistake in inflection or word choice could change the way you think about somebody. But I picked up on a lot of other things too — body language and what was behind someone's eyes.

We would go right up to people's houses and knock on their doors. This was the best way — catch people off guard, rather than bringing them into an institutional waiting room and having them sweat it out. There's another reason why a big interpreter is a good thing: the two of us were pretty intimidating.

But I didn't go for intimidation, generally. I just turned on the charm. With the women I'd flirt, and with the men I'd do the buddy-buddy thing. One day we had a house on our list that was in the best part of town in this little Bavarian burg. We'd been to some pretty nice houses, but this one took the cake. We rang the doorbell — those chimes that made you think you were in church. An ancient fellow answered, the butler. We asked to see the young lady of the house. Her name was Eve.

It was a beautiful scene. The house was dead white, the height of fashion at that time — the curtains, the rug, everything. It amazed me that places like that could remain untouched by all the horror around them. It was done in deco, so someone must have had good taste. We got ushered through a pair of double doors into a palatial sitting room with a view. We took two chairs opposite the double doors where we had been let in. The butler closed the doors, it was only a few minutes, and then she opened the doors herself and entered.

What can I say about Eve? In truth, I don't really want to talk about her at all. The whole thing is unsavory. That's the best way to describe it. I honestly didn't want to get into this. It was easy ranting about the psychiatrists. That's my usual thing, putting people down, stamping all over them, trying to come out of it without my feet too messy. I'm not going to do that with Eve. I have nothing bad to say about her — just the facts, which speak for themselves, I guess. But the problem is, I don't know what it all means. Up until now, I've known what everything I've ever written meant. This part is going to be unpleasant and embarrassing. And I don't want to alienate you; God knows I would never want to do that. But that's my vanity talking again. I *should* talk about Eve because I *don't want* to talk about her. Hell, I know you're a good friend and that you'll understand. Maybe you'll explain it all to *me*, because honestly, I really don't know what happened. I guess if you think less of me, that's the way it goes. Jesus, I've said goodbye to everyone else, if I have to say goodbye to you over this, then that's just the way it has to be.

The first thing I noticed was that she was completely in control. She had dark red hair, almost a maroon color. She opened the doors with a casual ease, and stood looking at us. The amazing thing about this whole process was that it took a lot of time, or seemed to. She did everything with enormous care, as if we weren't there. She was completely in the moment.

She was wearing a green dress. Why do I always remember the dress? It was the perfect color for her pale skin and her eyes. Later I realized they were flecked with green.

She gave us the once-over, then spoke. "Hello, gentlemen," she said in perfect English.

I could have gotten rid of the interpreter at that point, but I wasn't so sure I could handle Eve alone.

She came and sat on the couch opposite us. It was a huge white thing, and she sat in the very middle. She opened up a cigarette case, and took out a cigarette, and lit it. Then she gave us the once-over again. "How can I help you?" she asked.

You might think that as an interrogator, I wasn't doing my job, because she was so striking. But that's not the case. My senses were sharper than ever, *because* I was interested in her. I know I was a good interrogator that day, because it mattered more than anything for me to figure her out.

I did my usual thing, explaining why we were there and what we were up to. I remarked on her command of English. "I speak six languages," she said. And she didn't say it as if she was bragging. I asked for her name and age. She was twenty-eight, four years older than me. I asked about her occupation, and she said that she was an assistant professor at the university.

"Assistant professor of what?"

"Biology," she said.

We knew this already. We'd been told about the experiments that took place at the camps, and about Nazi eugenics, and though there was no indication that she had been doing work for the Nazis, we had to be sure.

I explained that we were formally arresting her, because

she was a member of the Nazi party. She didn't blink an eye-lash, and she didn't deny anything. She explained calmly that she was a low-level member. I asked her what that meant to her. She said it meant that she was from a wealthy family, and as a young Aryan woman, she was expected to join the Nazi party so that no one would question her race. This made perfect sense, and was most likely true. It didn't get her off the hook though. Everyone said this, and it didn't necessarily mean they were innocent. I asked her about her area of study and she gave an almost flip answer. "The sexual habits of mice," she said. I asked her what she meant by that. She said she had only been joking. I said I thought it was a pretty inappropriate place to make a joke. But I was damned impressed with her cool. She apologized, saying that the comment wasn't all a joke — there was a certain amount of truth in it. She said that she had been working lately on experiments with rodents, and it all had to do with sexuality. I decided to go right for the jugular. I asked her if she had ever made any experiments on humans. She said no, strictly mice. It was what she said after that, and the way she said it, that made me believe her.

She began to talk about her specialty, which was human fetishes and sexology. She said that before the war she had been working with someone named Magnus Hirschfeld. His work had been involved with the "relatively new" science of human sexuality. She had great affection for him, and for his work, but she realized that this was not a subject she could pursue under the Nazi regime. She had, however, continued to make contributions to the scholarly field, through her work with animals. I asked her if she knew anything about the types of experiments that took place in concentration camps. She looked at me with the interest of a scientist and asked, "What sort of experiments?"

She seemed genuinely curious. It was at this point I decided she was innocent. This happened often in the interrogation process. It's not just that I was romantically interested in her from the moment I saw her, it's that there's always a moment when you know, one way or the other. There's always a question that can be answered in two ways. One way will implicate the person completely; the other will get them off scot-free. If she had been guilty she would have immediately denied any involvement in the experiments. She would have acted innocent, trying to protect herself, saying, "Oh, were there experiments?" And then she would have said, "No, I didn't have anything to do with that — it's disgusting" or something. She would have tried to get the subject out of the way as quickly as possible, showed her horror and distaste, made a performance of it. But Eve did none of those things. Instead, she acted like a scientist.

This might seem grotesque to you. But you have to understand that to a scientist nothing is grotesque. It's the reason why we have the atomic bomb actually. For these people, science is all that matters; it's not their job to think about human implications. If scientists thought about the human implications of their job, then there would be no science, because science has a tendency to lead us into dark places, places we probably shouldn't go. Does this mean that scientists are evil? Probably. But it's not their fault. They're just doing their job.

I told her what we knew about the experiments. We didn't know much, but what we knew was horrific.

Unspeakable.

I spoke about it.

She listened calmly, and said, "But that would be unethical." Then she pointed out that such experiments would not be useful or scientific, and said, "There would be no point in me being involved with such things."

I believed her.

And it's important that you believe her too. The fact is: I became romantically involved with a member of the Nazi party. I did, and my father was a Jew. I don't care if you think what I did was unethical. Believe me, *I* don't. But it's important for you to believe Eve, and not think that I was swayed by romantic feelings. If you do think that, then suddenly this book will be about a Jew who gets involved with a Nazi. And that's not what it's supposed to be. I have to admit, I'm beginning not to know what it's about, but I do know it's not about that. Many, many more things happened between Eve and me that were, in some way — I'm not sure how — more important than the issue of her Nazi affiliation. I wasn't bewitched by her because she was "the enemy." I couldn't be bewitched by the enemy; I had seen what they had done, firsthand. She wasn't the enemy. What was clear to me from the start was that she was a completely honest, direct young woman, and brilliant to boot. She was speaking the truth, or at least what she perceived to be the truth. That was what attracted me to her — her incredible *presentness*, her lack of concern over what people might think of her. In a situation like this — where she was being interrogated and her freedom, perhaps even her life, were imperiled — it was almost impossible to believable that she could be so calm and frank.

The interview didn't go on much longer. I didn't see any point in interrogating her further, and I told her that she was no longer under arrest. It seemed to me that if she could be this honest with me, then all I could do was return the favor and be honest with her. Honesty was typical of all our exchanges after that.

The translator and I left for our next appointment.

Two days later, I asked her out to dinner.

I wish I could say I was tortured with conscience over the decision, but that's not true. I don't even wish that. I wasn't tortured. It's amazing, writing about her requires straight-forwardness — thinking about her again I don't know any other way to be. The fact that she was a Nazi didn't have anything to do with the delay. Like any guy in his right mind, I waited to call her because I didn't want to appear too eager.

I had never met a woman like her before. The only other woman I had been in love with was the daughter of a famous writer (I'm not going to name-drop here) who had hurt me badly a few years earlier. She went on to marry a famous actor who was three times her age, and that killed me. The girl was a sweet, innocent thing, not stupid; I'm not attracted to stupid women. The main difference was that until she dumped me I had been in control. There was never any doubt who was the man and who was the woman — who was *in charge*. I'd always liked girls like that, girls who I could put my arm around, and they'd put their heads on my shoulder and know it would be alright. Now, in Germany, for the first time, I'd met a girl — I don't even know if I could describe Eve as a girl, she was a woman — who might let me put *my* head on *her* shoulder. *Might*.

When I called Eve she was straightforward. She seemed a little surprised, but not too surprised. She said, "That would be nice," then asked if I wanted to see a performance of *The Merry Widow*. She said that dinner didn't interest her, and she always found it awkward to meet someone over a meal with nothing to talk about. Going to see an operetta would solve everything. I was pretty nervous, so it made perfect sense.

I didn't know what to wear, so I wore my uniform. She wore a black velvet dress. The show was in a beautiful old theater, and I met her at the door of her house. We took a cab to the theater. It was quite an event.

You could see that people were really trying to put their lives together again, acting like everything was normal. That's a completely human way to respond in a post-war situation. Hovich hadn't been hard hit — that is, none of the buildings had been harmed. And life went on as usual in Germany — just as it did in Britain and France — for those, of course, who were considered Aryan during the war.

Eve was excited about seeing the show. Not that she said it; I could just tell. She wasn't the type to get really excited about anything, at least on the outside — which was interesting considering what happened between us. On the other hand, I certainly don't want to give you the idea she was a passionless person; in fact, quite the opposite is true. That's what was so interesting about her. You could tell that she was excited about going to *The Merry Widow*, but she couldn't show it.

I've always been really sensitive to dishonesty, so you'd think this would have turned me off right away. It didn't. And again, it's not because I was attracted to her. I wasn't so much attracted to her at first, just very interested. But she wasn't hiding her feelings on purpose. She would never have done that. For some reason, and I'm not going to get psycho-analytical here, she couldn't be emotional. She wasn't a little girl who jumps up and down, and gets all excited about things. I've always been attracted to that type of woman, a woman who is more of a little girl, probably because I'm not the type to jump up and down myself — even though I jump up and down a lot inside. The cliché is true: people have a tendency to be attracted to their opposite. You tend to look for someone who will bring out things you can't express, things you can't do. What interested me about Eve was that she was somewhat like me, a good, honest person, but inca-pable of expressing emotion. It wasn't a matter of making a choice, of hiding something. She was clearly incapable of it. She might have liked to be capable of it, but that simply wasn't the case. I'm like that in a lot of ways. I don't want to be so antisocial, for instance. It's not a pretense; it's not some-thing I'm proud of. But it's the way I am, and I have to deal with it.

A lot of this had to do with her being a scientist. And you might find it odd too, with all the ranting and raving I do about Section Men, that I could be attracted to a scientist. It was odd, because science doesn't interest me much. But I don't consider scientists to be Section Men. As I said before, in the early part of this century the literature professors got jealous of the scientists. They realized that English wasn't taken as seriously as science, so they set out — completely wrong-headedly, in my opinion — to make it one. That's why there is such a thing as "English Lit" and why it's survived so long. But literature isn't a science; books can't be analyzed the way the world can, because a fictional book is the opposite of the world. I'm sure, for instance, that if this book was to be published, some Section Man would try to analyze it, and get a Ph.D. for saying what it "meant." But what it actually means is what it says. Unless I say I don't know what it means.

But I know you won't try to analyze this. That's why I let you read it.

Eve was not a Section Man; she was not someone trying to get rich and make a career by analyzing stuff that should be left alone. She was a real scientist, someone who was interested in the world and how it works. This was a pretty alien subject for me, but I respected her profession.

So there we were, in the cab. I let her talk about the play, because I could tell she was excited even though she didn't want to reveal it. Also, she seemed at ease talking about it. It all made sense to me. There's nothing I like less than fake conversation — talking about the weather. She told me what parts to look out for. It wasn't that she said, "Oh, you're going to love it when — whatever — happens." No, she just told me, rationally, as a scientist would, that there were certain key moments in the play. She mentioned, for instance, the reason why this particular operetta had been banned by Hitler. Apparently there was a song in it where somebody who works for the government rejects "The Fatherland" — the character actually uses that word — and instead goes out drinking. The song is all about how boring it is to do government work, and how drinking is better. She also pointed out that the plot of the operetta was pretty stupid — it was all about a rich widow and the men who were competing for her money — but that the music was exquisite. She used that word, "exquisite."

We must have looked pretty exquisite when we arrived at the theater. And it was an exquisite night, it really was. I was glad I wore my uniform because all the guys were dressed up like penguins, and the women were wearing ball gowns. It was like something out of a movie actually. That's what I remember most.

The excitement was palpable. (I don't like using obscure words like palpable, but I think you'll forgive me in this instance and understand that I'm not being pretentious; the word actually expresses the feeling of the place perfectly.) The rest of the people, unlike Eve, were definitely showing their excitement. You could sense the lid being taken off all that repression. This was a show they hadn't been allowed to see for ages, and they were completely enthused. Everyone was chattering, and all the women were throwing their heads back, and laughing, and holding onto their guys.

The show was amazing. Eve gave me the perfect advice. I couldn't understand much, which was probably a good thing. But I might have tried to figure it out if she hadn't warned me. The only time I had to ask her what they were saying was when one of the girls on stage made a remark, and the whole audience burst into laughter. It was obviously the highlight of the show. So I asked her what the girl had said, and Eve told me: "You're a horrible man, but a wonderful dancer." That's a pretty dangerous little line; I'm sure it's gotten more than one girl into trouble. That's why everyone laughed. But the music really was more beautiful than anything I'd ever heard before. The moment that Eve told me about — the hero is working at his boring desk and complaining about The Fatherland when he suddenly starts to sing about Maxim's — was one of the most beautiful melodies I'd ever heard. And I do understand that affection for bars. I've always wished I could have a favorite bar, like in Hemingway's *A Clean, Well-Lighted Place*. What Hemingway says there is that a good bar is one where you can feel totally alone, while still being around people. That's what I like about the *idea* of bars — the only problem is that I've never been able to feel alone in a place like that.

It was enchanting, but it was a strange type of relationship for me — suddenly I was an excited little boy, with an older woman who was enjoying my excitement, even though she didn't seem capable of expressing the same kind of excitement herself. Of course I wanted to kiss her out on the glittering balcony, but I didn't. I had a feeling that starting anything would have to be her call. After the show they kept the bar open, and we stuck around for a while and talked. Amazingly, I didn't hate anyone there. I figure part of the reason was that they were talking German, so I couldn't understand their stupid conversations. I remember thinking that it would be a good idea for me to live in a foreign country.

The fascinating thing is we ended up talking about God. Don't ask me how we got onto the subject, I can't remember.

But I do remember that Eve had a searching mind and loved exploring all sorts of topics. Anyway, God came up, and she said, "I'm godless." She looked at me with a challenging gleam in her eye. "I'm a godless woman."

I asked her what religion she had been raised in, and she said Lutheran. She asked me how I was raised. I told her that my mother was a Catholic and my father was a Jew. She laughed and said, "That's the worst."

I asked her what she meant and she said, "Those are the two worst religions. Such self-hatred. Such repression."

"What's so great about Protestantism?" I wondered.

"All religion and most excessive moralizing is a defense against death," she said, and then she went on and on about how Luther was the first rebel, tacking that sign on the church door and everything. I mentioned that I was writing a novel about a young rebel. She seemed to like that. At first it was hard to tell what she liked, but she was always interested. I was disturbed by her "godless" comment. My family hadn't been particularly religious, but my grandfather had been a rabbi before he became a doctor. No matter what you do, if your grandfather was a rabbi, there's going to be at least a lingering respect for God in your family. At that point in my life I hadn't yet discovered Eastern religion — but Eve's admission frightened and exhilarated me at the same time.

I asked her the usual question people ask whenever atheism comes up — about life after death. "I think you just die," she said. She thought it was typical that God and the afterlife were always discussed together. She said, "Doesn't it occur to you that God is just a reason to tell yourself there will be a comforting life after death?" The idea had occurred to me, actually.

"Don't you ever think about death, or worry about it?" I asked.

She said, "I think about it all the time. I have a bad heart." She told me she had a very rare disease called Wolff-Parkinson-White syndrome and that she could die at any moment. She explained that she had some extra passageways going to her heart, and that the electrical impulses could get rerouted, and start to spark off each other. "If that happened, it would be like this," she said. And then she did a completely uncharacteristic thing for such a calm and composed woman — she flailed about, her arms waving in the air, her head shaking. "It would be like that." Again, it was both funny and disturbing.

"I live with the threat of death all the time," she said, "I'm not afraid."

I was discovering that I never knew where Eve was going to take me, where her mind was going. Her sense of humor, as you can see, was dark and morbid. It wasn't exactly my sense of humor, but it fascinated me.

Since she was sort of in charge of things, it seemed natural for her to make the next date. In a wholly uncomplicated manner, she asked, "Would you like to get together again tomorrow night?" When I said I sure would, she suggested the cabaret.

If our first date was like a fairy tale, the second was the opposite.

I won't say it was a nightmare, because it wasn't such a bad night. I have to admit that I actually enjoyed it, very

179

much. But I felt like I was being pulled into something that I couldn't resist. I'm not going to say that Eve put a spell on me, because I don't believe in that sort of thing. But I know that if the second night had come first, then I might not have, eventually, married Eve. The first night was odd only for the moment when she pretended to die — but the second was strange from beginning to end.

The cabaret was a little like the famous one from the movie — except it wasn't really like that at all. Eve asked me to meet her there, in the basement of an old building on a deserted street. It was a small, dilapidated place. The tables were of different sizes, some wooden and some metal, and they were all covered with different fabrics, which made it colorful, if inconsistent. The tables also had lamps, which were connected clumsily to an outlet on the front of the stage. There were different kinds of Persian carpets on the floor, which covered most of the lamp chords, but you had to be careful because the carpets were bumpy. The stage was tiny. It wasn't made out of wood or anything; it was a natural rise in the cement floor, a higher level of the basement. The performance area was probably only about ten feet square, because there were clothes racks at the sides, piled high with costumes.

But the first thing I noticed was the mural on the back wall.

It was copied from the popular children's book *Babar*, and it was, technically speaking, very well done. The colors were bright and the illustrations looked as if they had been traced, only on a much larger scale. The problem was what the elephants were doing. You probably know *Babar*. It's a cute story about elephants that get into all sorts of adventures. There are mother elephants, and father elephants, and baby elephants — the whole thing. In this mural, the elephants looked great, but what they were doing wasn't exactly cute. I'm not going to go into detail, but I think you get the idea. It was obscene, and it was made more obscene by the fact that when you first looked, you thought, "Isn't that sweet?"

The hostess led me to the table where Eve was waiting. The hostess was polite and everything, but made me nervous. Maybe it was the mural that set me off, I don't know. First, she was ugly. She had overly large teeth, hardly any chin — had she been in an accident? — and bony shoulders. Her dress was too shiny and falling apart in all the wrong places — like under her arms. But she was enjoying showing herself off. In fact it was that — the idea of showing off something that no one should be proud of, that characterized the place. The cabaret had maybe thirty tables, but only half of them were occupied. Maybe because it was a too warm night in October — everyone seemed to be sweating. I know I was. Most of the couples already seated were a little too fat and smiled a little too much, in the same way the hostess was skinnier than a healthy person has a right to be.

Eve was wearing a very different kind of dress than the night before. It was red and satiny and left little to the imagination. Actually, it was obvious that she was naked underneath the dress — that she hadn't bothered with underwear. She was having a drink and smoking. She acknowledged my discomfort, but not in a condescending way. She asked, "Are you frightened?" I told her that I was, a little bit. I wouldn't have been able to answer her so honestly if she had taken pleasure in my uneasiness. This was a key aspect of our relationship. Eve was always teaching me, but what made it bearable was that she never treated me like a student. It's as if everything was just as new to her, and she was experiencing it for the first time. Obviously she had been here before, but the way she treated the situation was as if she were frightened too.

"You never know what's going to happen," she said.

There was an emcee who, when I think about him now, reminds me of the movie *Cabaret* as well. The difference? Joel Grey was slick and witty. You couldn't exactly call this guy either of those things — just like you couldn't call the performers talented. It was a freak show. The emcee was older and not pleasant to look at it, though he seemed nice enough. The problem was that he was displaying lots of his saggy old body through his tattered tuxedo. He said he had been bombed. There were a lot of jokes like that — Eve translated — which made me glad I wasn't in uniform. Eve explained that the cabaret hadn't been operating during the war so people were just starting to enjoy it again. Even though there weren't a hell of a lot of people present, the ones who were there seemed to be in on the joke, and now and then they would yell out to the emcee. I asked Eve what was going on. She said that most of them were saying, "Take off your shirt!" It was a horrifying thought. The last thing I wanted to do was see any more of the guy's pasty, hairy body.

It only got worse. The first guy to come out — I didn't really get him. He was, again, very ugly. Most of the people in this show were ugly, even the women. He was messy, and overweight, and smelly-looking, and seemed half-asleep. His stutter reminded me of the Army psychiatrist. He talked for quite a while, slowly, and people laughed now and then. I asked Eve what he was saying, and she said he was talking about falling in love. But what were they laughing at?

"He's retarded," she said.

I didn't quite understand why that was funny, but it was impossible for me to judge because of the language barrier. I know it sounds like a horrible thing to do — laughing at a retarded man talking about a failed affair. But the people were laughing with him, not at him. At least he seemed to enjoy it when they laughed — like a retarded stand-up comic.

The second and third acts were simply unforgettable.

A tall woman in a black dress was out next. She had slicked-back, dyed black hair, and she was wearing a tie — it looked odd with the dress. The emcee said a few introductory words. Then he brought out a bunch of what looked like bicycle horns, all lined up in a row. Then a circus podium — the kind a seal sits on. It looked authentic, right out of the circus. The woman knelt on the podium and started to blow the horns to play a tune. As I remember, the tune was "On Top of Old Smokey" — which I thought was strange as it was an American song. As it turned out, the whole piece was a political comment. When she finished each part of the tune the audience clapped, and she revealed her hands, which had been hidden by the long sleeves of her dress. Or maybe I should say her lack of hands — she had stumps. Then she barked, and slapped her stumps together, like a seal would slap its flippers. It sounded like the slapping hurt.

I was dumbfounded. I'd never seen anything like it in my life. The audience didn't laugh at her, they were appreciative. There was an intermission, and I asked Eve what it was about. She told me that the woman had lost her hands during an American bombing raid. Then the piece made sense. I could understand why it would mean something to these people. You might think it would have made me angry, as an American, but it didn't. I had nothing against the German people; I could understand why they would be angry about being bombed. The only thing most of them were guilty of was electing a bitter, crazy, megalomaniac — which is something we're all guilty of from time to time.

During the intermission, Eve also told me something about her personal life. She asked me if I had ever been married, and I told her about the bad experience with the girl who ended up marrying the world-famous actor. To her credit, she wasn't the least bit impressed when I mentioned his name. That kind of thing didn't seem to interest her at all. Then she told me her story. She had been married once before, but she didn't want to talk about it. She simply said, "He was inferior." I know that statement sounds ruthless. It is, but it was also the truth as she saw it. I'd certainly had a lot of experiences with inferior people, and I could see that Eve was a superior person. I didn't see it as a horrible thing to say, it was a fact. It gave me a pretty clear picture of him right away. It was as if she was saying, "Let's face it. We judge people, you and I. And why shouldn't we? Why should we waste time with people who have nothing to offer?"

The third act took the cake. They dressed the set during the intermission, and there was a little cot in the corner all made up to look like a pretty fairy bed, pink and gossamer. It was odd that the bed was so small though. I didn't know what to expect. The lights went down and music began. I recognized it right away: "In the Hall of the Mountain King" from *Peer Gynt*. When the lights came up, there was a little person pretending to be sleeping in the bed. Then she slowly woke up. At first I thought it was a little girl, and then I realized it was a midget.

She was probably a dwarf. Midgets — as I understand it — are perfect small humans. This woman had a very large head and very fat legs; she was physically misshapen and dressed in a little fairy nightgown — with wings and everything. She pretended to wake up, as if she'd had a long night's sleep. Then she started to get ready for her fairy day. Except it didn't look like it was going to be a traditional fairy day, because she took off the nightgown to reveal a bra and panties, and then put on fishnet stockings and high heels. You couldn't help laughing, in spite of yourself. The thing that made it so funny was the music — it was the troll's song after all. I don't know if she picked it herself, but it was absolutely perfect. It brings to mind little trolls, busily getting ready for the day — and here she was, a little troll, doing just that. At the song's climax, when the music goes crazy, she finished dolling herself up in a miniature hooker's outfit. She then performed an obscene dance, shaking everything.

It was like watching a train wreck. You had to look, but at the same time you felt you shouldn't. To her credit, Eve wasn't sitting there monitoring my responses. I glanced at her once or twice and she was totally immersed in the show. Everyone thought it was fabulous, a real climax to the evening, and the fairy dwarf dance got a couple of curtain calls. When the lights came up, Eve asked me what I thought. I told her that I didn't really know what to say. She shrugged and said, "Be honest." I said I was fascinated by the whole thing, but that I felt guilty. "Why?" she asked.

"Isn't she being exploited?" I asked.

Eve said, "No, she's a prostitute. The money she gets for the show means she doesn't have to work tonight."

It made sense, but it was a bit much for me. I didn't have a hell of a lot of experience with prostitutes, and certainly not dwarf prostitutes who performed in bars.

At this point the whole thing became embarrassing, and I don't even know if I want to go on. I certainly want to make sure that you understand that I'm telling you all this because I think you should know everything. And I have to tell myself again that I shouldn't care what you think. But I care about you, and I don't want to lose you as a friend.

———

I'll try to get to the point. What happened next was that Eve invited herself to my apartment. This made sense. We obviously couldn't go to her place. She lived with her parents, and, as she had told me, they were old and conservative. I knew what the invitation meant: Eve was initiating the physical part of our relationship. I expected her to do it — I had been waiting for her to do it. In this way, *I* was like the blushing bride. She was being clear about the fact that she wanted me; I wasn't used to dealing with women like that.

Our intimacy was unlike anything I'd ever experienced. In bed she was exactly the way she was in real life, matter-of-fact and controlling. I'll have to admit this drove my libido crazy. When you're with somebody like that, it's like they're always a mystery; you can never figure them out. You want to make them go as crazy as you are, but they never do. You want to get right under their skin, but you can't because they are controlling you, and, I guess — to some degree — keeping you at a distance. But I also understood that this was the closest Eve would ever get to revealing her true self.

I was hooked. And I don't mean to suggest the relationship was all physical, or that Eve had me in her thrall. That's far too melodramatic. I was hooked because I'd never met such a fascinating woman before, such an intelligent woman, someone I could respect absolutely, without the slightest doubt. I never for one moment thought that she had a single fault. I found nothing to criticize. She was not only smart, she was logical. There was a reason for everything she did. She went to the operetta with me because she loved the music, and she thought it would be a good thing to talk about — period. She took me to the cabaret because it was part of her research into sexuality. I respected that too. But it's important for you to know that I never felt like part of an experiment. When we were in bed, she was as honest as she could be.

She was perfect for me in other ways too. At the time, I had a lot of doubts about my writing. My fear was that if I met the woman of my dreams, I would stop writing my novel. A lot of writers worry about things like this. It's irrational, of course, and when I expressed the concern, she quickly talked me out of it. She told me that there were things about me that would never change — this was true of everyone — and my need to write was one of those things. She told me there were dark places inside me and they would never go away, and that I didn't have to worry about becoming too content. Eve had no use for conventional psychoanalysis, and she wasn't interested in sexology because she wanted to "cure" people. She wasn't interested in fixing me, she loved me the way I was. She talked a lot about society and intolerance. Eve was right; when I was with her I did some of my best writing. But I was also concerned because I knew some people might find my novel shocking. It was a big problem for me. I would never set out to shock anybody; it's the last thing I want to do. I don't think shock is a good thing in itself — it's shallow and doesn't lead people anywhere beyond surface emotions. But what was more important was that I didn't *want* to upset people. A lot of my earlier stories had a cuteness about them — it's one of the reasons why I don't like people reading them now — and one of the reasons why the *Saturday Evening Post* bought them in the first place. I knew the novel wasn't going to be "cute," that some people might not like it, and might even be angered by it. I don't like making people angry. I don't consider myself an iconoclast. What a stupid, fake thing to boast about. But Eve said it was foolish of me to worry about what people *might* think. I was a writer first and foremost and should write what I thought was best. She also loved what I had written. She was actually as close to becoming passionate about it as I had ever seen her. When she was passionate about an idea, her eyes began to sparkle. It was a physiological fact. I don't know what the scientific explanation would be, but I swear it happened. You could see that she was almost bursting, even though her voice stayed calm.

So I found a woman to love, who not only supported my work and helped me in my writing, but absolutely understood it. I was convinced she understood it better than I did. She wasn't an artist; she was a true critic — not the kind who tried to psychoanalyze me, and was bitter and mean about my work — the kind who loved my fiction and understood it in ways I never could. I think there were things she wasn't telling me about my writing because she knew it wouldn't be good for me to hear them. Not bad things. But Eve was so smart she understood what every critic should understand — that there are ideas a critic may have about the work that a writer should never know.

Our affair went on like this for a few months before I proposed. I knew our job in Germany was done, and that it was time for me to go back to America. I wanted to take her with me — I knew I didn't want to live in Germany. I'm too American, as much as I hate the people, and the politics, and everything. Don't ask me why, I can't explain it. I didn't think she would want to come. After all, she was so German. Her acceptance took me by surprise — everything about her did. But she told me that she was interested in the papers being published by American sexologists, and she talked about Kinsey, who had published some interesting work on wasps. I didn't know what she was talking about at the time, but I was ecstatic that she wanted to be with me. We had an interesting discussion about the Marx brothers too. That's the way she described America, "The home of the Marx brothers — so crazy, so perfect, so human!" I'd always loved the Marx brothers, and we talked endlessly about their antics. I told her my favorite thing was when they met a buxom older woman. She said that was one of the most interesting things about the Marx brothers. She said that they were sexual perverts, all of them, and that's what made their work vital. I was disturbed by the remark, but years later I read an interview with one of the Marx brothers in *Playboy* — I think it was Harpo — and he talked about their offstage antics. Yes, they were always chasing women in real life, and yes, they were obsessed with the physical side of love. Eve was right. Again.

We had a quick little civic ceremony in Germany. I was glad to get it over with. I never looked forward to the ceremonial part of things; and Eve was so logical about everything that it didn't mean anything to her. But then we had to face reality: where would we go when we got stateside? Neither of us had much money. I met her parents and they were as Eve described. They spoke only German, so I didn't really have much idea what they were saying. They seemed cold. Eve claimed they liked me in their own way, but I didn't believe it. Anyway, Eve wasn't going to get any of their money until they died, and she wasn't too sure she would get any of it at all after marrying an American soldier. So we were penniless. None of that mattered though — we were in love. But it meant that in the good old U.S. of A. we would have to live with my parents.

Now I really have to tell you about my parents.

I never wanted to write about them; it's too personal, and I know how people speculate. But I have to, and I can't help but think that you'll judge me. Eve would tell me not to care, and I shouldn't. I can't help but think you're judging our marriage. I know you're thinking we were involved in some sort of weirdness. And to some degree, you're right. You might even be thinking Eve was a sexually perverted Nazi. If you are, you're wrong. The way I look at it now, everything happened for a reason. Eve was presented to me — like Treblinka — to teach me something about myself. I'm not saying Treblinka was all about me, I'm not that self-centered. What happened was Eve showed me something about myself I needed to know, something that really scared me. At first it seemed like an adventure in self-exploration, but when we arrived in America it became a nightmare. Our relationship wasn't like it was in Europe, and I know why.

A lot of it had to do with my mother.

I can't go on about my mother without sounding a little crazy. She was special — her one fault was that she loved me too much. I know that her relationship with my father wasn't very rewarding — or maybe the best way to put it would be that he wasn't really capable of giving affection to her, or anyone. But he was a strong force in our household, and my mother really loved him. It was a hopeless love, the kind I respect. She was always making excuses for him, apologizing, and making things right. "It's not something your father can say out loud dear," she'd tell me, "but you know he's proud of you."

She doted on me, and I know she loved me more than she loved my sister. That's a horrible thing to say — but what could she do? I was her little man — I guess I was all the things my father could never be, I had all the sensitivity he didn't have. But she never criticized my father. Her attitude to her marriage was the same as my attitude to the war: it was a job. I don't mean to suggest that she didn't love my father. In fact, deep down, I think she was most attracted to his aloofness. You can psychoanalyze that and say that it's sick, but Jesus, we do the best we can, don't we? We try to love, but nobody is perfect. People are generally horrible, so if you find someone you're capable of loving even a little bit, it's best to stick with them.

Until I was about fifteen, I thought my mother could read my mind. It came, I guess, from her reactions to people. She could see right into someone's heart instantly, a talent I got from her. You couldn't lie to her, it was impossible. She was so friendly and sweet, no one could have known how judgmental she was. I don't blame her. She could see through people, and what she found wasn't pleasant. When we used to have people over to dinner for my father's business, my mother was funny. After these evenings were over my father would retire right away — being social really wore him down. When the guests were gone and my dad was in bed, the fun would start. My mother, and my sister, and I would sit around talking about everyone. My mother could be terribly cruel, and we loved to pick people apart. From an early age, this confirmed for me the idea that my mother and I were special. By her early teens, my sister used to avoid these hen parties, they became too much for her. She started to think my mother was nasty. I never thought of it that way, or, I guess I should say, yes, she was nasty, but I loved her for it. This was the best time for my mother and me, when we just had each other, and I knew that we had exactly the same opinions about things. We would even set traps for our guests sometimes, and watch people walk into them. It wasn't cruel because no one knew what we were doing — the people were never embarrassed or hurt, but we knew, always.

But something happened when I was sixteen: I started to notice girls. My mother, being so critical, never seemed to approve of anyone I had a crush on, and I realized pretty quickly that no girl I brought home would please her. So I began to distance myself from my mother and her opinions. I never actually disagreed with her, but I started to absent myself, and I know that hurt her deeply. There was no one for her to gossip with. There's no doubt about it, a kind of pact was broken. The daughter of the famous writer never met with her approval, and I probably never would have gotten involved with her if I had listened to my mother. The galling thing about all this is that she was right.

I know you're thinking that my mother wanted me all to herself. How can I make you see that's not true? When I made it clear I needed my own space, she gave it to me. My mother was not the kind of sad person who would have wanted me to stay at home and take care of her. She wanted me to have my own life. The war got me out of the house for a couple of years, but even after the whole Eve thing was over, I stayed. I couldn't stand it though, the old pressure was there: to think like her, to confide in her. I had to move out and get the little black apartment, but I never lost respect for my mother. It was never about emotional greed, never about selfishness — it was always about truth. There's old Ramakrishna again. I can't ever think badly about someone who is compelled to speak the truth.

When Eve and I got back, we walked into a den of vipers. Not that my mother was venomous — but the emotions hissing under the surface were. On the one hand, I always respected my mother's opinions, but on the other it was important for me to make my own choices and express my love for Eve. You could say that it was all about asserting independence — but that would be too simplistic. You must understand that as much as I distanced myself, I still respected her. And there I was, with another woman whose opinion I also respected. It meant more than anything for them to get along.

And they did, at first.

If it was hard to tell what my mother was thinking, it was even harder with Eve. My mother was always so nice, so charming, but Eve never betrayed the slightest emotion. She wasn't the least bit nervous about meeting my mother: maybe it would have been better if she was. I don't think my mother had met anyone like Eve, ever.

Because we were married, my mother insisted on putting us in the same bedroom. This makes perfect sense, what else would she do, give us separate bedrooms? And naturally, she put us in my old room, with all my school pennants, and my rock collection, and the *Timmy Books*. Like lots of mothers, she had touched nothing in that room since I left. I would have preferred to stay in my sister's room, and then maybe the memories wouldn't have come flooding back. I tried, but my mother wouldn't have it, and I didn't want to make a scene. In my sister's room, I might not have thought so much about being a child again in my mother's house.

wasn't like that. She wasn't a meddling busybody, and she recognized that even though she was my mother, I was a grown man. She knew it wasn't her business to tell me who to marry. And she didn't do anything sneaky or subtly manipulative either. That also wasn't like her. At first, I really had no idea that she didn't like my wife. But then the two of them had an exchange that made it clear — and Eve said the wrong thing.

We were sitting around after dinner — my father had gone to bed early, as usual — and my mother started talking about the mole on her neck. She had a mole that had gotten bigger, and it was looking pretty ugly and scary. She knew Eve was a doctor and a scientist, and I'm sure that by bringing it up, she was hinting that she wanted Eve to take a look at it. She wasn't laying a trap — I knew what it was like for her to do that, I had seen it too many times. She was simply worried. Now my mother was indicating pretty obviously how she wanted Eve to react. Like anyone in this situation she was saying, "I'm sure it's nothing. I'm being a hypochondriac, there's really no point in getting into a state about it. It's just a mole." And Eve, figuring that my mother was worried, asked if she really wanted her to examine it. At first my mother told her not to bother, that it was no big deal. Eve didn't force the issue, but said, "I think maybe you'd like me to take a look, to reassure you."

Ultimately, this was the worst thing she could have said — because my mother agreed. I think my mother believed that Eve really would reassure her. And just like my mother wasn't laying a trap, neither was Eve. I think she figured that my mother was being a hypochondriac, and it would turn out to be nothing. Even if it was a bad sort of mole, I'm sure she felt my mother would be able to handle whatever she said. So Eve had a look.

My mother said, "It's nothing, right?"

And Eve said, carefully, "I don't know. I'm not a medical doctor. But it couldn't hurt to have it looked at by someone else."

I could see the pain and fear in my mother's eyes. It wasn't as if she hated Eve, or blamed her. It was one of those instances when you want reassurance, not *truth*. No one could blame my wife for what she said — it was completely in character and not at all malicious. She was concerned and only trying to help. I don't think Eve had any idea what had happened — my mother was that good at hiding unpleasantness. And Eve wasn't the type to worry about what other people might be thinking. She hadn't done anything wrong — on the contrary, she had responded to my mother's worry in the only way she knew. She was being truthful, logical, scientific.

The incident passed, and Eve went to bed. We were in the habit of *not* going to bed at the same time. It wasn't a ruse; we were a newly married couple and it was pretty evident what might be going on in my old bedroom. But I couldn't stand the idea of going into that room *together*. My mother and I did not talk about the mole. She probably asked me about the progress of my novel, or about my publisher. But I had a feeling and I had to ask her about Eve.

I shouldn't have. But I need to make it clear: what she said didn't have much to do with my decision.

It certainly wasn't the only reason that I split with Eve.

But it was a contributing factor.

When my mother said she was tired and going to bed, I

asked her, casually, "So what do you really think of Eve?" Of course, it wasn't really a casual question; it could never have been casual. My mother sat down again. She paused and pressed her hands against the thin material of her dress. I'll never forget her hands.

"She's very beautiful," she said, "very accomplished. She's a remarkable woman. I can see why you are in love with her."

I knew this wasn't all she would say. Suddenly I was a teenager again, and the hapless guest had departed. We were going to share a confidence about a stranger — to look into their heart. How did I get myself into this? I knew I should never have asked, but I couldn't resist.

"Is that all?" I couldn't believe the sound of my own voice.

"There is one little thing," she said, "that makes me a bit uneasy."

"Oh," I said, trying to sound relaxed. "What?"

"She doesn't like Jews."

The words made a dull thud. I felt as if a brick had hit me in the chest.

The problem was, she was right. Like Eve, my mother was always right.

But she wasn't right in the way she thought she was. It's true, Eve didn't like Jews. But she didn't like Catholics either. She didn't like any sort of religion. I tried to remember if Eve had made this obvious — I couldn't think of a moment when she did. I could have gone into an explanation. I could have explained that Eve was an atheist, not a racist, and that the kind of accusation my mother was making was completely unfounded. And though being an atheist would have been less offensive to my mother than being a racist, she wouldn't have liked that much either. My mother wasn't a staunch Catholic; in fact she had changed her first name to a more Jewish one when she married my father. But she had never become a Jew. There wasn't a lot of talk about religion in our house. But on the other hand, none of us kids had ever talked about being "godless" either. And since I didn't defend Eve, allowing a lull in the conversation, my mother dove right in with the most wounding comment of all. "And you can't forget that you're half Jewish —"

And then she spoke my name. My whole name, not my nickname. I never liked my first name; it's a very Jewish name. Actually, I think it was right then that I decided to never, ever use it again.

My mother was right, I often conveniently forget about being Jewish. And my Jewishness is a truth. But in a way, it's not.

I didn't think much about being Jewish, but not because I was ashamed. It was irrelevant to me, as irrelevant as it was to Eve. The damage had been done, however, the words had been spoken. I could tell she felt guilty for having said them. "It's just a little thing though," she said. "I'm sure it doesn't matter."

She kissed me goodnight and went to bed. I was devastated. It wasn't something I could tell Eve about; my mother had forged a secret bond between us, against Eve. If I had told my wife, she would have dismissed the comment as typical of non-Germans. She would have thought it had no basis in fact — and it didn't, really — and so it wouldn't have bothered her.

You might think it's a contradiction, that I've said that both my mother and Eve were right in their own way, and that both were speaking the truth.

That was my dilemma.

I was upset by what my mother had said, but I did not fully realize the implications. Or maybe it would be more accurate to say that her comment wouldn't have had any implications at all except for what happened next.

When I got back to the bedroom, Eve and I started doing what we did every night since our second evening together.

Here's where things start to get really unsavory. It was the climax of everything — the trip to the cabaret, Eve's godlessness, her distance, her obsession with science and truth. There was a mirror in my room above my dresser, like in most little boys' bedrooms. It had my favorite Cub Scout pins, and other things decorating it. On one side, I had pasted the cover of my favorite childhood book, the one about the pig's "dilemma." The tape used to hold it had long ago disintegrated, but somehow it still held. Well, that mirror had become, at Eve's subtle insistence, a part of our lovemaking. God, this is so awful. At one point during the games that night, I happened to look into the mirror, and I saw myself. . . .

I won't tell you what I saw, but it was so disgusting, so appalling — I was . . . The best way to describe it is to say that I was red-faced and debased.

I couldn't believe what I was doing.

That was it — the turning point. I saw myself, and what I was capable of, and it seemed as horrible, in its own way, as the things I had seen in the war. Of the body, completely — a place where sex and death sit cozily, like old friends, having a lethal chat over tea.

I didn't say anything to Eve; I continued on with the game.

We went to sleep and woke up the next morning and had breakfast with my mother. My father left early each morning. After breakfast, my mother decided to go shopping. It was one of her rituals. My parents lived in the nicest part of town, on the Upper East Side, and one of the rewards of that area were the extravagant jaunts she made to the best stores.

When I was alone with Eve, I said it. It wasn't difficult. I was so ashamed, so convinced that I had become another person, because the part of me I had discovered with her could not be me, that — I can't say I hated her — I hated myself. And the only way to stop hating myself was to get rid of her as soon as possible. I said, "Eve, it's over."

"Where does this come from?" she calmly asked.

"I just . . . I can't," I said.

I was too ashamed to even speak about what I'd seen in the mirror. There was a long pause — it seemed long, but I don't know how long it really was because it was one of those moments when things don't seem real — and she said, as if stoically accepting a harsh truth, "I see. Your mother doesn't like me."

"No, that's not true," I said, because it wasn't.

"Don't lie to me," she said. But she didn't get angry — she never got angry.

"I'm not lying."

"There's no point in lying," she said again, not with contempt, but with her familiar, cool, collected logic. She went to the bedroom and started packing.

It took her a while to arrange to leave America — we must have stayed in that room together for at least another week. I don't know how we did it.

I wasn't worried about her; Eve had been married before. Maybe she would tell the next man that I was "inferior." Eve wasn't the type of girl you worried about.

After that, my life became a repudiation of everything Eve stood for. Eve was science, logic, the truth that comes from the empirical world — from our senses. She was the body. I would be the opposite; unscientific, illogical, the truth that comes from pure fiction. The truth that comes as a hallucination after you have starved yourself nearly to death.

———

I don't want you to think of me as a mystic; I don't see myself that way. It would be nearer to the truth to say that, simply, I love fiction.

But I can't go on like this. Not after what I've said.

I have a feeling that I'm going to lose you as a friend.

Because that's what this has all been about — having you as my friend. You know it, I know it. It's what the critics always used to say about my books: the problem was that they were too personal, that the narrator *was* me. My books were from the heart, really from the heart, so the critics called them sentimental. Because I was speaking directly to the reader — and that was a bad thing.

Why?

A good book isn't something they *tell* you is literature — you should feel the breath of the man who wrote it.

Okay, I admit it. This is a letter to you. All my books are letters. And yes, that's why I always read what my readers write to me. Sure enough, now and then, there's a landsman, someone who knows, who understands, who laughs in all the right places, who can't bear to finish the book, and who can't bear to finish *me*.

Reading a book is like falling in love.

It's all out now.

You're supposed to love me. No, more than that, you're supposed to love me unconditionally — *because* of everything that's wrong with me. You're supposed to love me for my worst. Isn't that what everybody, deep in their heart of hearts, really wants?

If you turn away from this — that's the way it goes.

───

I was at the local restaurant the other day. I had to get out. I found myself making a fuss over the rice pudding. And I thought about the wispy waitress who, so many years ago, complained about the cranky old man who made such a fuss over the same thing.

I am that cranky old man now.

───

I'm sorry I mentioned the war. Chekhov used to say that if a gun is mentioned in Act One of a play it has to go off in Act Two — or else it's a bad play.

The war was a gun and it had to go off.

I'm still sorry. I really am. But the truth has to come out and you have to try to love me anyway.

I know, I already said that.

———

When I was in prep school I was involved in an amateur production with a local theater group. I played a girl. And I was
good at it. There was an older man in the play, and an actual
teenage girl too. Sometime during the run of the play, the old
man fell in love with the girl, whose name was Diane. He had
a lot of scenes with her, and, at one point, had to kiss her on
the cheek. When the play was over, he lost his mind for a
while, and also lost a lot of weight. I met him once at a greasy
spoon downtown — a very Edward Hopper sort of place.
He'd been wandering around. He told me that he had written
a hundred-page poem about Diane, called "The Dianead." He
wanted to read it to me. He was looking for a place to perform it too. He said that if he read it in public, then he could
invite Diane and she could hear it. He asked me if that would
be a good idea. I said to him, "If you were eighteen years old
and a sixty-year-old man wrote a hundred-page poem for you,
wouldn't you be a little bit intimidated?" He looked at me
blankly, with softly questioning eyes, "Do you think so?"

———

I was not made to live in this world. I'm better at things I
think are true but aren't. If you can figure that one out then
. . . write me or give me a call.

———

For reasons related to my will, I had to phone New York

recently. At least I didn't have to go there. Nothing could have been more painful.

Officious women, they will be the death of me. I was cranky. Frankly, I don't have much charm left.

All I needed was a number, a special number, and in order to get it I had to give her my full name — middle name and all. I was hoping she wouldn't know. Maybe she hadn't read a book ever in her life. Sometimes I pray for those people — the stupid, illiterate ones, who couldn't possibly have heard of me. I suppose I should congratulate myself on becoming a pop culture figure — even those who have never cracked the spine of a book recognize my name. Anyway, after I gave her the whole thing she repeated back to me the abbreviated form. "Is that you?" she asked. Did she have any idea the agony it caused me to answer her? It was pretty obvious she didn't. I gave up trying.

"Yeah, that's me," I could barely get the words out.

"It's *interesting* to talk to you," she said, slyly. But she didn't mean it as a compliment. I had been short with her. I had proved myself faithful to the stereotype: a bitter, crazy, famous person. She couldn't wait to tell her friends. After all these years I shouldn't be bothered by incidents like this. But it still takes me a day or two to recover.

—

To all those who have betrayed me: don't worry, you're not going to rot in hell.

—

Riding the bus to Dartmouth, the same bus on which I met Pegeen, a slender boy sits in the seat in front of me. His hair is dyed blond and brilliantined. I guess they call it gel these days. It's pretty obvious he's on his way to the big city. There's so much hope in the gleam of that hair.

A woman reads a story to her child. Really self-satisfied. She's confident that this sanitized story is perfect for her little innocent. I tried to read the original Grimm's to my kids but I didn't have the heart. Like every parent, I wanted to protect them. But there's no point. They see worse on TV. So, instead, you get so angry, you just want to grind their face in all the horror.

See what's coming? See?

But there's no point in that either. They'll find out in due time.

———

The truth is, I like you and I don't want to say goodbye.

The feeling is mutual, I know it is. It must be.

So let's sit down, have a coffee. You tell me what's up with you, I'll tell you what's up with me. There will be all the betrayals of the day, the little embarrassments.

You will laugh and shield your eyes, then look up at me. I will be captivated by the kindness, the inexpressible sadness.

You get it, that's all that matters. You *get* me.

———

When I was young my mother told me to clean my room once.

"You know, I was worried," she said many years later. "You cleaned it up too well. It was too clean."